Fire AND Wings

Fire AND Wings

DRAGON
TALES FROM EAST AND WEST

Edited by *Marianne Carus*

Illustrated by *Nilesh Mistry*

with an Introduction by *Jane Yolen*

Cricket Books
Chicago

Table of Contents

Introduction
Dragons: An Unnatural History
by Jane Yolen

Oh, how I wish dragons roamed the earth today, fire-belching monsters a hundred and fifty feet long, with hard green scales and long serpentine tails. Flying monsters with names like Tiamat, Apophis, Fafnir, Tarasque, Naga, and Lung.

There were the Western dragons who lived in caves and guarded their enormous amounts of treasure stolen from the countryside around: gold-stemmed cups, ruby bracelets, diamond tiaras, opal-studded torques, amethyst brooches, silver belts and buckles and spurs. These dragons lay upon their hoards, waiting to devour a passing maiden.

Or there were the Eastern dragons who lived up in the clouds, masters of the growling storms, bringers of the gentle rains, masters of the waterways: of rivers, lakes, ponds, seas. They could even make themselves small enough to fit into a raindrop. These were the dragons of whom the Chinese said, "The small dragon is a caterpillar; the large dragon fills heaven and earth."

Dragon stories can be frightening, full of blood and fire and sacrifice. But they can be quite beautiful, too, when they are of sacrifice, redemption, bravery, and love.

The old Roman writer Propertius told the tale of a ceremony in a town not far from Rome, which was under the protection of a dragon who lived in a slimy pit. Each year a single maiden was chosen to be lowered in a basket into the pit, where she was to hand-feed the monster without flinching. It was said that if the girl was pure of heart, she would be returned safely, and for the next year, the crops of the town would grow well.

But why should I—like J. R. R. Tolkien, the creator of *The Lord of the Rings* and *The Hobbit*—say "I desire dragons"?

Because there is something seductive, something wonderful, something both scary and enlightening about dragon stories. Humans have told such tales from the very beginnings of time. There are dragon stories from ancient Mesopotamia and in the Bible as well. There are dragon tales from long-ago Germany, Norway, France, Libya, Italy. Dragon legends have been repeated and retold since the earliest Chinese civilizations, and that is a very long time indeed. Hundreds of dragon stories, even thousands of dragon stories, can be found in the old traditions.

So with all of the old tales about dragons, why write new ones?

Because many writers desire dragons, too.

In a dragon tale, the modern writer can put the tenderness of father and son as in Patricia MacLachlan's lovely "Dragon's Coo"; or the bravery and cleverness of a soldier can be discovered as in Eric A. Kimmel's Ukrainian-based "The Three Riddles"; or the skill and hardiness of a young girl can be shown as in Phillis Gershator's "Kotoshi the Dragon Doctor"; or the prowess of a maiden disguised as a young man can be recounted as in Teresa Bateman's "The Dragon at the Well."

Maybe we can't have real dragons roaming the earth, fire-belching monsters a hundred and fifty feet long, with hard green scales and long serpentine tails. Flying monsters with names like Tiamat, Apophis, Fafnir, Tarasque, Naga, and Lung.

But in our stories—both old and new—these dragons live, they fly, they fight, and sometimes, they die. In so doing, they touch the magic spot deep within us that does, indeed, desire dragons.

Fire AND Wings

The Dragon at the Well

by Teresa Bateman

Prince Peter rode through the forest, cursing the heat and the tangled pathways that led nowhere. He'd been lost for days, and it seemed as though all the gold coins in his pouch could buy neither a drink of water nor directions home.

"It's your fault," he muttered angrily to his horse, but the tired animal only sighed and plodded on.

Suddenly a walled fortress appeared through the trees, its gates open. Peter rode into the silent courtyard and dismounted at the well. As he raised a brimming ladle of water to his lips, he was startled to see an owl launch itself from the wall. What was an owl doing out in daylight? Peter's eyes followed the bird's flight to where an even bigger surprise waited—a dragon.

"Drink, and you must pay the price," said the dragon.

"Price?" Peter quickly regained his composure and flung his belt pouch at the dragon's feet. "I am Prince Peter. I can pay any sum you name." Again he raised the dipper to his lips.

"Gold is not the price," said the dragon.

"Then what?" asked Peter impatiently.

The dragon smiled. "I ask for your firstborn daughter."

"Is that all?" laughed the prince, stooping to retrieve his gold. "You ask little enough. Consider the bargain struck." He drank deeply from the well, emptying the dipper twice before allowing his weary horse to drink.

When Peter turned to ask directions, the dragon was gone. He noticed, though, that a road wound through the forest beyond the fortress gates. Wondering how he had missed it, the prince mounted his horse and followed the wide, smooth track back to his castle. Once safe at home, he soon forgot all about the bargain he had made.

Years passed. Peter became king, married, and rejoiced at the birth of two sons. Then a daughter was born, and his heart sank. He gazed into the baby's eyes, so like his queen's, and remembered everything. Desperate, he devised a plan to save his daughter from the dragon.

The king and queen named their child "Prince Merin" and raised her as a boy. She learned archery, swordplay, and dragon lore. She swam in the moat and became skillful at chess.

Her mother made only one demand—that Merin not cut her hair. "A princess's hair is her crowning glory," the queen insisted. "Let's not forsake her heritage entirely." And so it was that Merin's hair was braided tightly and covered with a cap.

Sixteen years went by. The princess's laughter filled the castle, and after the queen died, Merin was the only one who could make her father smile.

One hot summer day Merin was shooting arrows in a high-walled courtyard. Sweat trickled down her nose. Alone, except for a small brown owl, she removed her cap and let down her braids. Her father would disapprove, but he need never know, unless owls could talk. What was an owl doing out in daylight anyway?

A flurry of wings launched the bird into the air. Startled, Merin watched as it seemed to shimmer and disappear.

"Must be the sun," she murmured, returning the cap to her head. But the harm was already done.

Suddenly the air was battered by great wings.

Merin's hat flew off again as a jeweled talon plucked her from the ground.

Her father was watching from a palace window, but he could do nothing. Within seconds, the dragon was high in the air and shimmering out of sight.

At first Merin beat at the clawed foot with her bow, but it was futile, and soon they were circling down toward a fortress surrounded by trees. As they landed in the courtyard, an owl settled on an open window. Released, Merin spun around.

"I'm Starler," said the dragon. "Welcome to your new home."

Merin looked around her. Stone walls rose tall and forbidding. "Why am I here?" she asked.

Starler eyed her speculatively.

"Your father long ago promised me his firstborn daughter for a drink from my well. It's a price he seemed willing to pay at the time, but I see he's tried to cheat me."

"So I must pay the price for my father's foolishness?" she asked.

Starler motioned her inside. "Come, eat. Then I'll tell you the price of your freedom. Pay it, or serve me the rest of your days."

Seeing no choice, Merin obeyed, but she couldn't help saying, "You'll be disappointed in my housekeeping. And if you think to eat me, I suspect I'll sit ill on even your ironclad stomach."

Starler laughed as a well-laden table appeared.

"I don't lack for food," he remarked.

The owl Merin had seen in the courtyard swooped down, snatching a piece of meat off the table.

"Did I introduce you to Whirland?" the dragon remarked, shooing the bird away with a wing tip. "He's been my only companion since . . . well, for many years. It seems most creatures fear dragons, and my lot would have been lonely without him. I send him where I will, and he brings me news of the outside world. Still, he could improve his manners."

Merin smiled as Whirland landed on the dragon's wing to eat. The owl's trusting nature made Starler seem less threatening. Even so, the dragon's next words were daunting.

"You may serve me," Starler said, "or win your freedom. Every midnight I have a visitor—a cocky lad who's never been bested by any man. Defeat him in three contests, and you will be free."

Merin considered. "What kind of contests?"

"Chess the first night, to test your strategy, then swordplay the next night. If you survive, you will be allowed to choose the final contest."

It seemed she had little choice. Merin agreed to the tests.

That night, as the clock struck twelve, a knock came at her door. She took a deep breath and swung it open, unprepared for the charming young man who stood before her.

"My lady," he murmured, startling green eyes looking into hers. Under one arm was a chessboard.

"Call me Merin, and what may I call you?"

"Thomas the Undefeatable."

Merin raised an eyebrow. "Indeed? I'll just call you Tom."

Tom put the board on the table, spilling the chess pieces out. Merin quickly chose white, looking for any advantage she could gain. Tom raised an eyebrow, but said nothing as he set up his dark pieces. His confidence was unnerving.

Merin played well, but for each move Tom had a countermove. After trying familiar gambits and finding them thwarted, Merin cautiously attempted new moves. She would not allow herself to be pushed into indiscretion.

Tom kept up a lively banter, but it faltered as the game wore on.

Merin yawned, then blinked. Tom had nudged his king with a thumb, surreptitiously moving it a square. She glared, and he nudged it back. Merin was heartened. If he was trying to cheat, he must feel threatened! She moved her queen, creating an opening for him to attack an apparent weakness.

Dawn was near when Tom fell into Merin's trap. She moved her knight. "Checkmate."

He looked shocked. "Well played, my lady. But can you handle a sword as well?" He bowed, then was gone.

"Wait!" Merin shouted, running after him. But the corridor was empty.

The evening after besting Tom at chess, Merin dined with Starler. She was surprised to find herself laughing more than once at his dry wit. Starler's stories about griffins and dragons were so delightful that she was almost sorry to see the evening end.

As midnight neared, Merin returned to her room to find a sword on her pillow. She swung the weapon, delighting in its balance, but she was sobered by the thought of the contest ahead.

When the expected knock came, Merin flung the door open and saw her opponent of the previous night. Now he wore an elaborate suit of armor, but no helmet. He smiled, his eyes filled with anticipation . . . and dread.

Merin had no time to ponder this as she thrust forward to join battle. She quickly established a pattern, and Tom followed it. Thrust, back step, left thrust up, right, sideswipe left. She led her opponent down the hall in a deadly dance.

Merin found her training tested to its limits and began to tire. She stepped onto a rug, leading her opponent across it. Thrust, back step . . . Tom pressed forward as she faltered. She stepped onto stone floor again, and her sword dipped in apparent defeat. Tom lunged just as she snagged

the rug with the point of her blade and flung it up to catch his sword, bringing it crashing out of his hand.

He stared in astonishment, then bowed. "You have won again, my lady."

"Tomorrow the choice is mine," Merin snapped. "Bring a bow and arrows. We'll see if your archery is better than your swordsmanship."

Tom gave her a strange grin—mixed delight and defeat—and ran down the corridor and out of sight. Merin sank to the cold stone floor and leaned her forehead against her knees. One more night, and she would be free.

The next evening as she and Starler dined, Merin realized how much she enjoyed debating with the dragon. Their viewpoints often varied, but conversations were never dull. Besides, there was something in the dragon's gaze that tugged at her heart. Merin quickly put that thought away, not wishing to analyze it further.

As the meal drew to an end, Starler rose from the table. "Tonight is the final test," he said. "If you win, you will be free."

"I'll win," Merin said firmly.

"Then I wish you luck," said Starler. "I must go now. Tonight will be busy, and tomorrow . . ." There was an awkward pause, and then he was gone.

Merin went out to the courtyard to prepare for the archery contest. Curious, she tried the outer gate. It opened at her touch. Freedom was a footstep away—but what of honor? She turned back to the courtyard.

The full moon provided light, while the abandoned stables supplied moldy hay bales, grain sacks, and paint. Merin drew targets on the sacks, draped them over the hay, and hauled the bales out into the courtyard. Mice, disturbed from their peaceful homes, ran over her toes.

"Sorry," Merin grunted, "but this hay will soon prove very inhospitable."

She turned to find Tom watching her. Leaning against the well beside him were two bows and a quiver of arrows.

"Are you ready?" he asked.

"I suppose I'm as ready as I'll ever be," she replied.

The contest began, and Merin was dismayed to find they were evenly matched. Their arrows landed so near each other that it seemed neither would win.

As the full moon slid westward, the two opponents stopped to catch their breath. Merin noticed a mouse poking its nose out of one of the hay bales. Foolish thing not to have gone when it had the opportunity. Perhaps she had been foolish, too.

"It's nearly dawn," Tom announced. "You haven't won. Therefore, you've lost."

Just then Merin saw a movement on a window casement. "See that owl?" she asked. "Whoever can bring him down will win."

"I can't shoot Whirland!" Tom said.

"Are you conceding the contest?" Merin asked quickly.

Reluctantly Tom raised his bow and took aim, but at the last moment his arrow flew wide. He watched uneasily as Merin placed an arrow on her bowstring and aimed at the owl.

He started to speak, but she shook her head. "My freedom is at stake."

"And mine," Tom said enigmatically.

She pulled the bow taut, then suddenly dipped it. The arrow hit the stones at the heels of the mouse poking around the targets. Startled, it ran. Whirland saw it and swooped low over the courtyard, touching down briefly as he caught his prey and rose to the window again.

Triumphant, Merin turned to her opponent. "I brought the owl down, just as we agreed. I've won."

Tom was leaning against a wall, relieved. "I actually thought you were going to kill him. I should have known better."

Merin frowned. "Do you admit defeat?"

"I stand fairly defeated," he said.

There was a ringing of bells. The moon slid behind the trees as the sun turned the sky pink-gold. Merin watched, fascinated, as the empty courtyard suddenly came to life. Vines wound their way up the walls, and horses stamped in the stables. People laughed inside the fortress. Outside, the ancient forest seemed to step back as the gates swung open.

Confused, Merin turned to Tom. He was smiling a

strangely familiar smile. "You did it!" he said, swinging
Merin off her feet. "You've broken the enchantment!"

"What enchantment?" she asked. "And where's
Starler?"

Tom flushed, then after a moment said softly, "I am
Starler. And before that, I was a cocky young prince who
refused to help an old man in need. When he threatened
me with disaster, I declared, 'I can be bested by no man!'"

Tom avoided Merin's eyes.

"He cursed me and the fortress. I could only walk as
a man from midnight to dawn. During that time, if I
could be fairly beaten in three contests of wit or skill,
the curse would be lifted. But my own words were used
against me. I could be defeated by no man."

"And when you were a dragon?" Merin asked.

Tom gave a wry smile. "The dragon could grow in wisdom, and did. The man stayed much the same—certain
of his own abilities and unwilling to admit defeat.

"It was your father who gave me hope," Tom continued. "In him I saw my own faults—he was untrustworthy,
proud, overconfident. I suspected he would break his
promise and raise his daughter as a prince. It's what I
would have done. And while it's true I could be defeated
by no man, *you* are not a man."

His gaze made her blush. Looking into his eyes,
Merin could see the same quiet wisdom that she had
grown to love in Starler.

"Now," Tom said, "you've won your freedom, but I've lost my heart. Will you stay as my wife?"

Merin nodded. "I will, if only to improve your chess game."

The wedding was planned, and Merin sent an invitation to her father, with no mention of the bride's name. His sons urged King Peter to accept, hoping to break the sorrow that had held him in its sway since the death of his queen and Merin's capture.

A carriage came to take him to the wedding. On arrival, King Peter didn't recognize the fortress he'd visited so many years ago. Nor did he recognize the bride, resplendent in a flowing gown and veil, her long hair cascading over her shoulders.

He stepped out of the carriage, tired and thirsty. The bride herself hurried to his side with a dipper.

"What would you give to quench your thirst?" she asked.

"I would go thirsty the rest of my days," he choked out, "if I could but undo the bargain I struck so long ago."

Merin smiled, although tears filled her own eyes. "Father," she said, lifting her veil.

Unbelieving, he looked up into blue eyes so like those of his late queen. Merin placed a hand on his shoulder.

"Drink, Father," she urged. "The price has been paid."

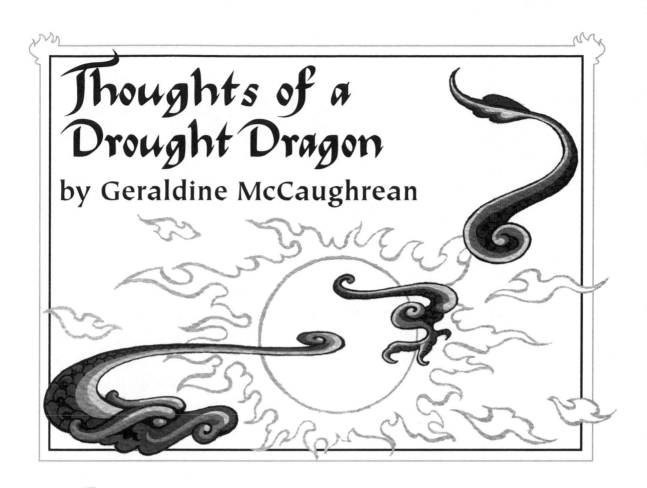

Thoughts of a Drought Dragon

by Geraldine McCaughrean

The Yengee River is yellow, but its spray is white. The people who live on the cliff overlooking its waters say that the river once swallowed a dragon. The white spray is the dragon's smoky breath. When the sun is low in the sky, the dragon's fire turns the yellow water red.

The Yengee Province is old, and the story is older still. When it was first told, the blue glaze of the mountains was barely dry on the porcelain sky of China. The Yengee had only one village on its banks. Behind its houses, the brush strokes of its paddies were vivid and lush, the hibiscus flowers full of bees, the cranes' long necks as serried as the bamboo thickets.

Then late one summer no rains came to tarnish the copper heat. The young shoots crisped, the white clouds curdled, the yellow river shrank, and the farming people of Yengee wiped their faces with their hats and said, "Drought!"

"It is well known," said the magistrate, "that rain clouds are formed from the breath of storm dragons. Since there are no rain clouds, it follows that we need a dragon."

So the people of the village set about building a dragon, as their grandfathers had done before them in times of drought. They constructed a frame from whippy bamboo, and each of the overlapping scales was a pointed bamboo frond. They set it on wicker paws and gave it a wicker basket for a head. Its eyes bulged with red peony flowers—tight, red balls of petal.

"What a handsome beast!" said everyone, standing back and laughing. "What a ferocious monster!"

But no rain came. The dragon was lifted on poles and danced between the houses and across the fields, firecrackers banging in its wake. The shortest pole was held by the youngest dancer—Haoyou—who was allowed to dance beneath the great flowery head, making the lop jaw sag and snap and chatter. It was hot work, but so proud was Haoyou that he danced as energetically as any of his brothers or uncles or neighbors. Soaked in sweat and as thirsty as July, the dancers danced from dawn till long past noon . . . but still the sun blazed and no rain fell.

So the people of Yengee decided to destroy the dragon.

"If it won't breathe out rain clouds," they said, "let its smoke rise into the sky and become a rain cloud. Tomorrow we shall burn it."

As the elders of the village discussed the failed dragon, Haoyou, exhausted, curled up just where he was inside the dragon's snout. He fell sound asleep. Soon the rest of the village was sleeping, too.

Within the hollow hive of the dragon's head, the words hummed like bees—hummed and swarmed and stung. The Drought Dragon flexed its six wicker paws. Its leafy hackles rose. Its chrysanthemum ears swiveled, and its hibiscus horns shed pollen like dandruff. The tail, tipped with raw silk, *rick-racked* as the firecrackers had done, and cracked itself ragged. Finally, the tightly closed peony eyes began to open, petal after petal folding away from the dark heart like a thousand vermilion lids.

"Is it rain they want? Then I shall give them rain! I shall refresh them with showers of ash! Burn me? I shall give them a *firestorm!*"

Just then, inside the dark recesses of the basket head, little Haoyou turned over in his sleep.

Aha! thought the Drought Dragon with its wicked wicker brain. Already I have swallowed one of them without even trying! Crispy rack of peasant! Char-broiled dancer! I shall roast and eat every one!

Haoyou opened one eye. Thoughts like hornets whizzed by him, ricocheting off the bamboo laths, pinging off the flower stems. But Haoyou's wits moved just as quickly.

"No, no!" he said aloud. "Do you not recognize the stirrings of *conscience?* Listen! I am the voice of your conscience!"

Sadly, such notions were beyond the Drought Dragon. "Nonsense! Dragons have no conscience!" it said. "They are all heat and anger and energy!"

Haoyou knew this was true, for he was inside, and Heat and Anger and Energy swathed him round. The dragon had begun to cough up sparks as sharp and shocking as firecrackers. Haoyou's rice-straw jacket began to smolder, his hair to shrivel. He had to think fast or the dragon would burn first him and afterward his home and every home around it. Even now the dragon was running toward the village. Haoyou had to run, too, or be dislodged from his hiding place and trampled by the hind feet.

"What are you thinking of?" he bellowed, giving a sharp jab with his short pole. "Fool dragon! Do you know nothing of your own history?"

The dragon came to an abrupt halt so that Haoyou cannoned into its sinuses. It rubbed its itchy hide against a stone wall, which promptly collapsed. "History?"

"You are made of flowers, aren't you?" said Haoyou. "Flowers from a garden? Don't you remember what you were *doing* in that garden? How you came to be there?"

The dragon searched its no-brain for memories of its past, but found nothing other than a headache behind its eyes. "I only know that I shall burn the garden and the houses round it and the gardeners, too!"

"What? You don't remember hopping among the chrysanthemum flowers? Singing on the peony bushes? Nesting amid the bamboo? Don't you remember how those wretched peasants made your soul . . . from a *nightingale?*"

The dragon thought so hard that its head filled up with soot. "No. But if I was ever a miserable little bird, I'm glad not to be one anymore!"

Haoyou kicked off his straw sandals, which were starting to char. "Ah! But to have lost the power of flight! That is a terrible thing—especially for a dragon."

Even the tears of a dragon are not cool. They fall like molten gold dripping from a crucible. "To fly! Ah yes! To fly!" sobbed the dragon. "I do wish I could do that."

"Maybe you still can?" suggested Haoyou.

So the dragon tried to fly. It hurtled through the sleeping village, dragging and ragging its silken tail behind it, jumping, stretching out its neck, thrashing its no-wings. The red-hot anger inside its head only grew with every failed effort.

"It's just that you've grown so much bigger," said Haoyou, gasping for breath. "But if you were to launch yourself off the cliff yonder . . . maybe then you could get airborne."

If he could just persuade the dragon to throw itself from the cliff, it would plunge to destruction in the gorge below—a pile of bamboo bones on the riverbed, some blood-red petals, a small boy inside its broken head. At least the village would be saved, and that was surely worth the life of one small and insignificant boy? With fingers and toes, Haoyou clung on inside the wicker head, bounced about until his bones rattled, trying to think dragon thoughts—only dragon thoughts, nothing but dragon thoughts.

But Haoyou had reckoned without one thing: dragons have no fear. *Fear* is not in their vocabulary. Boys, on the other hand—oh! boys have fear! And the smaller the boy, the greater the fear, however brave that little boy might try to be.

Suddenly, the dragon found its skull full of fear. Though it shook its head till hibiscus petals flew in clouds, though it rattled its snout till its snail-shell teeth fell out, the dragon could not dislodge the fear. In fact, the closer it drew to the cliff, the greater the fear grew, until at the very last second, the dragon dug in its bamboo claws and skidded to a halt, head lolling over the precipice, peony eyes staring down. Haoyou, clinging on inside the wicker skull, looked down, too, and his stomach turned somersaults like a Chinese acrobat.

"Why can I not fly?" asked the dragon, even angrier than before. "I shall just have to go back and burn down the village, as I planned!"

"NO!" cried Haoyou involuntarily.

"Why not?"

"Because you . . . because . . . you still haven't used your bird magic!"

"Bird magic?" The dragon scoured its no-brain for knowledge of bird magic but found none—until Haoyou supplied it.

"Well, *singing*, of course! Everyone knows that birds sing before they fly! That's the magic that lets them fly. *Tut-tut.* Don't you remember anything from your days as a nightingale? All you have to do is sing!"

The dragon gulped in a breath. It inflated its bamboo ribs, flexed its fronded diaphragm—then sat down. "I don't know how."

"Yes, you do! You do! You do!" cried Haoyou. "Repeat after me: *Tweet-tweetie-tweet!*"

The dragon opened its mouth. Fire, like a broken oil lamp, belched out of its hollow nostrils. A thornbush caught alight.

Haoyou gave a groan. Perhaps this had been his most stupid idea yet, for now the tinder-dry grass would burn, along with all the rice shoots, the straw houses. Unless . . .

The dragon began to sing. *"TWEET. TWEETIE-TWEET-TWEET,"* hoping for bird magic, hoping to fly.

Far beyond the Yengee hills, the storm-cloud dragons lifted their heads, drowsy from hibernating overlong. They tottered to their feet, snapping at shoals of fire-flies. Again the noise came that had woken them, and they cocked their fronded ears. It was the cry of a dragon —not of their own breed but unmistakably a dragon.

The Drought Dragon sang, and as it sang, the bamboo bands of its body twanged like a three-stringed *qin*. Haoyou sang, too—any and every song his mother had ever taught him—songs for planting, songs of threshing, counting chants and skipping rhymes, lullabies and laments. Flame from the dragon's snout seemed to be setting fire to the very darkness. "Look up! Lift your head!" shouted Haoyou, but the dragon was too busy singing.

Haoyou slipped out of the skull and in under the jaw, lifting it with his short pole and all of his small strength. He must direct the plume of fire into the night sky and away from the brittle, brown grass.

He no longer knew what the dragon was thinking, for he was outside its head.

Over the crest of the mountain they came, indiscernible at first—the same color as the peaks. But then, as dawn rose, their strange colors became plain: the color of bruises, from purple to sickly yellow and every shade between. The storm dragons and the rain clouds they breathed out were vast. They moiled and toiled their way across the sky, intertwining and separating, their growling growing to a sound like distant avalanches.

When the Drought Dragon saw them, it stared. It stared and stared with boggling peony eyes, until the first raindrops fell with violent energy onto those crimson eyeballs. Chrysanthemum petals fell in sodden clumps to the ground; bamboo leaves gleamed sweat-wetly. The hollow nostrils gave off hissing steam as they filled up with rain: teeming rain, battering rain, torrential, soaking rain.

As Haoyou ran home, his bare feet splashed through deep puddles.

And yet, for all the rain that fell that day as the storm dragons stampeded across the sky, the monsters grew no smaller. Toward evening, Haoyou splashed his way back to the cliff and swept the litter of bamboo, leaves, and petals over the precipice, into the river below. Shielding his eyes against the rain, it was plain to him that one extra storm dragon had joined the herd even now thundering away over the eastern horizon, soaking the thirsty land as it went.

Dragon's Coo
by Patricia MacLachlan

Once, in a deep wood beside a field of wild asters, there lived a dragon. He was a leftover dragon; leftover from old battles with long-ago knights, leftover from quiet lurks about ancient castles, leftover from the great forests with the tall trees and dark caves. He lived, lonely, in the wood, away from everything but the birds and his animal friends.

There were two things this dragon wished for most in the world. He wished for a name—his own had been lost in the long ago. And he wished for a family.

"A family," he called to the birds who nodded and chattered noisily at the tops of the trees. Birds had families each year. Sometimes two. They knew everything there was to know about families.

"A name?" asked the weasel and the fox who lived behind the big tree and under the gray stone. A name, they pondered.

"What about Dromo?" asked the weasel, who was good with words. "Dromo dragon. It has a ring."

"It doesn't ring for me," said the dragon, shaking his large head.

"What about Rex?" suggested the fox.

The dragon shook his head again.

"Or Wiley?" said the weasel.

"Or Red-Tail?" said the fox.

"Or Marcus?"

"Or Elliott?"

"Or Blanche?"

"Blanche," said the dragon, drawing up quite tall and trying hard to remember past days. "Blanche is a girl's name."

"It doesn't *really* matter what name you have, you know," said the weasel, who was very hungry. He ran off into the underbrush to forage for food.

"You will know," said the fox, who was very wise. "You will know when you hear the right name." And he followed the weasel into the forest.

So the dragon was left alone in the wood, beside the field of wild asters, with no name and no family. He had the sky and the forest and his friends. But the only thing he owned was a round rock ball, smooth from years and years of rolling beneath his feet.

It was the very next morning, clear and cool, that the dragon found the babe. He might not have found it at all if the old round rock ball hadn't rolled down a small hill, under an alder bush, and bumped against the babe, who cried out.

It was a new sound to the dragon.

"What was that?" he asked. He turned around carefully and looked beneath the bush. He saw the bright eyes, the nose, the tiny mouth. The babe sat up, the blankets falling around his small body like petals of a flower. The dragon's heart beat faster; his body felt warm.

The babe looked up at the dragon and smiled.

"Mine," said the dragon suddenly. "Mine."

"Coo," said the babe, staring thoughtfully at the wondering dragon.

"It's a coo!" shouted the dragon happily, causing the leaves of the tree to shiver. "It's a coo and it's mine!"

The birds swooped down from the trees and flew about nervously.

"What is a coo?" they sang. There was much talk among them. They, like the weasel, the fox, and the dragon, had lived for so many years in the depths of the forest that they had no idea of how a babe looked.

"There is a cuckoo," murmured a mourning dove. "Perhaps there is such a thing as a coo."

"My coo," said the dragon, smiling.

"A coo?" asked the weasel, skeptically sniffing about the babe's head. He jumped backward—fearfully—as the babe reached out to touch one of his ears.

"A coo, you say," said the fox warily. "I've never seen such a thing." But the hair that had stood up along his back settled down comfortably. "If you say it's a coo, then a coo it is." After all, the fox was very wise.

Dragon cared for his coo the best he could. He fed him the wild blooms of the daylily and the tender leaves of the wood sorrel. He gathered sweet berries and wild nuts, carefully cracking the shells beneath his great feet. He sheltered the coo from the rain and snow, standing above him with his long head bent down, always watching. And he kept him safe from danger, knowing the wildness of the wood.

The coo grew older and stronger. He learned to cup his hands to drink the cold spring water that dripped between his fingers and ran down to his elbows. When he walked on two feet for the first time, there was great celebration. The weasel was pleased because he, too, could walk on two feet. The fox was fierce because *he* could not. The birds, of course, walked on two feet when they

walked at all. And the dragon cared nothing but that he loved his coo.

More springs passed, and the dragon grew older, too. Faster, it seemed, than the coo. The dragon slept longer hours—long past sunrise. And he lay down again before the evening light had gone behind the forest trees.

The coo, who was now taller than the fox and weasel and as wise as both, began to care for his dragon. He brought the dragon food, washed him with cool spring water when he was warm, and wove a pillow of leaves, twigs, and pine needles for his head.

And the coo began to learn about sounds. He heard the warning sounds of the birds, the commanding sounds of the fox, and the hunting sounds of the weasel. But most of all, he heard the loving sounds of the dragon. He listened and began to weave all the sounds together into a language all his own.

One day, when the dragon was stiff and weary, the coo brought him a meal of berries and wild fruit. The coo touched him gently. He looked at the long body. He brushed his hand along the kind face.

"Papa," he said softly. The sound, sitting strangely on his tongue, was like a burr, there to try again. "Papa," he repeated, and his breath touched the face of the dragon like a caress.

The dragon opened his old eyes and turned to look at his coo.

"Listen!" whispered the weasel. "Did you hear that sound?"

"What does that mean?" cried the fox excitedly.

"Papa?" repeated the dragon, wonderstruck, his old eyes shining. "I do not know."

But as he reached out to touch the face of his own coo, the dragon knew two things. He knew he needed no other name than that which the coo had given him. In it, he had heard the sound of love. And with that love, he had—at last—a family all his own.

Si~Ling and the Dragon

by Joan Hiatt Harlow

Once, in the land where mornings begin, a good emperor ruled for many years. But like all things earthly, one day he died, and his subjects mourned. His young daughter, Si-Ling, grieved with her mother at their great loss.

The court officials gathered to discuss who would become the next ruler.

"Alas, the emperor has left us only a daughter," said one official.

"We must search the land for a new leader, someone who will rule with the soul of wisdom," an elder statesman said.

"First, he must be tested by the great dragon who dwells in the mountain," the wise old mandarin reminded them. "It is the custom. Already smoke is rising, and the mountain shakes. The dragon is waiting."

"Who will dare to face the dragon?" the counselors asked themselves. "The dragon speaks with fire and can devour anyone in the flash of a flame."

Si-Ling, the young princess, who had been standing silently by the door, approached the group. "I shall face the dragon."

The counselors shook their heads. "You are just a child—and a girl."

Turning away from Si-Ling, the mandarin said, "We will search our country for a courageous leader who has the soul of wisdom."

The next morning, a proclamation requesting fearless young men to appear before the court was sent throughout the land.

But no one came.

"There is no one who dares to face the dragon," the wise mandarin said with a sigh.

Again Si-Ling approached the gathering. "*I dare.*"

The officials consulted with one another and finally decided that Si-Ling should go on her quest.

The following dawn, Si-Ling went to her mother, who sat by an open window in her quarters, as she had since the emperor's death.

"Mother, the kingdom will go to another dynasty

unless I journey to the mountain and meet with the great dragon."

"If you fail, Si-Ling," her mother said tearfully, "you will never return."

"I will not fail," Si-Ling promised.

Her mother's face was as sad as a broken flower. "Be careful, my daughter, and come back safely," she murmured.

At the city wall, the old mandarin was waiting. He unlocked the gate that led to the Mountain of the Dragon. Si-Ling looked out at the smoking mountain.

"The cave of the dragon is there." The mandarin pointed to a jagged cliff. "Beware, my child."

Si-Ling waved good-bye and walked toward the overgrown, rocky path that lay before her. After a long climb up the mountainside, the trail became steep and less trodden. Down in the valley she could see one small village. Finally she came to the wall of a cliff and could go no farther. On the rocky face of the mountain was a gaping hole: the cave of the dragon!

A rattling roar shattered the silence as the dragon slithered out from the cavern, its green scales shimmering in the sunlight, its eyes like burning coals.

"Who dares to walk onto my mountain?" As the dragon spoke, flames erupted from its mouth, and the very ground beneath Si-Ling's feet quivered.

Si-Ling drew herself up. "It is Si-Ling, the future empress."

The dragon laughed, and black smoke billowed into the sky, darkening the sun. "So the emperor has left a girl to rule after him? What makes you think you have the courage and wisdom to rule your people?"

"I had the courage to come to your mountain," said Si-Ling with a deep bow. "Now I will show you that I am wise enough to rule."

The dragon slapped its tail on the rocks, and scales flew like sparks. "You have demonstrated your *courage*," it conceded. "To prove your *wisdom*, I shall give you three riddles to solve. If you do so, you will become the chosen ruler. If you fail . . ." The dragon howled, and the sound echoed over the mountains.

"Tell me what I must do," said Si-Ling bravely.

The dragon was silent for several moments. Then it spoke with a voice like echoing thunder. "First, you must come before me, walking a tiger in the clouds." The dragon turned and disappeared into the darkness of the cavern.

Si-Ling left the mountain and wandered down into the valley. Where will I find a tiger? she wondered. And how can I walk it in the clouds? Surely this is an impossible quest.

She made her way to the nearby village, hoping someone would help her.

The villagers told her of a fearsome tiger that once stalked nearby. They said that the beast was as long as a sea serpent, with pointed claws and teeth as sharp as the

dragon's fangs. Surely Si-Ling could never tame that wild creature!

Later, Si-Ling walked in the countryside near her own home. She looked longingly at the distant palace. How could she face the dragon without an answer to the riddle? Worse yet, what would happen to her if she failed in her quest?

In a field, children gathered around a beggar who worked with paper and sticks. "Go," he said, handing each child a colorful kite. "Go, soar with the wind. See how beggars' children can fly above the royal palace itself!"

The children darted through the windy meadow, shrieking with delight as the kites flew high above them.

Si-Ling bowed courteously to the beggar. "Before the

sun rises tomorrow, I would like you to make me a kite," she said, "a magnificent kite that I will describe to you."

The poor man's eyes lit up. "It is done," he agreed.

The next morning, Si-Ling spoke to the dragon, who peered out from the darkness of the cave. "Watch and see how I walk a tiger through the clouds." Then she went to the path that wound around the open edge of the cliff. In her arms she held a bundle of colorful, striped paper with a long string. Si-Ling grasped the string and began to run. The paper crumpled behind her, then it filled with wind, expanded, and rose into the sky. Higher and higher it flew. The string tugged in her hands, but she held tight and raced along the path.

A majestic tiger soared above her, bobbing with the wind, dipping and rising into the low-hanging clouds.

"Look above you, Great Dragon," Si-Ling called. "See how my obedient tiger walks through the clouds for me."

"Yes, you have indeed solved the first riddle," said the dragon. "But there is a second one for you to solve. Put out your hands."

Si-Ling held out her small hands.

"How tiny they are! Can they guide an empire?"

"They are the hands of a woman. They will rule with gentle strength," Si-Ling answered. "Now, please tell me the next riddle."

The dragon spoke, and Si-Ling could hear the sound of storm winds in its voice. "You must bring me ten thousand trees—in the palms of your hands."

"Honorable Dragon," Si-Ling protested, "what you ask is impossible."

"Wisdom makes all things possible," answered the dragon. "If you are to rule, you must solve this second riddle." The dragon hissed, and smoke billowed around it. Again the cliffs shivered, and the mountain quaked.

"I shall find the answer," Si-Ling declared.

She took the path down the mountain and through a forest. Tall pine trees towered above her, blocking the sky. They whispered softly in the afternoon wind, and their tangy scent refreshed her. She placed her hand on the trunk of a tree. No one can carry even a single tree, yet the dragon demands ten thousand, she thought.

Beyond the forest was a field where she spied one small tree that was laden with golden red pomegranates. Si-Ling was hungry and tired from her journey, so she plucked one of the pomegranates and sat down on the grass. The sky above her was like blue silk, and the sun was beginning to set. Si-Ling pulled off the hard rind and bit into the sweet fruit. She ate eagerly, the juice dribbling down her chin as she sucked the hundreds of luscious seeds inside.

Night began to fall, and the moon rose like a lantern. Si-Ling lay down on the grass, gathered her robe around her, and closed her eyes while the stars glistened above.

When dawn came, she awoke with joy. "The answer has come in my dreams!" She plucked a pomegranate from the nearby tree and returned to the dragon's cave.

The sun was high in the morning sky when she reached its lair. "Dragon!" she called.

The dragon pushed its huge head out from the cave. "Where are the ten thousand trees?" it demanded. "Have you come with empty hands?"

She pulled the pomegranate from her robe. "I have brought you ten thousand trees," she replied. "Here in the palms of my hands is a fruit with hundreds of seeds. They will become hundreds of trees with hundreds of fruits with hundreds of seeds. Ten thousand trees and more will grow from this one small fruit." Si-Ling smiled and said, "I have solved your second riddle, Great Dragon."

"True, but a more difficult task is ahead," the dragon warned. "You must bring me the most precious of all jewels."

"I have many jewels," said Si-Ling.

"You may choose from all the gems on the earth. But I will accept only the most precious."

"I shall return to my home," Si-Ling told the dragon. "That is where I will begin my search."

The mandarin opened the gate as Si-Ling approached. "Have you completed the quests of the dragon?" he asked.

"I have yet one more. The dragon demands that I bring it the most precious of all jewels."

Si-Ling returned to her room and opened her own jewel box. Rubies, emeralds, and diamonds caught the light and sparkled inside. A white jade, carved with flowers, glistened like the moon. They were all lovely, but which was the most precious?

"Here is a diamond, the oldest and most durable of stones," she said to herself. The diamond glittered, scattering rainbows around the room.

She held a gem to her eye. "This emerald is as green as the dragon itself."

She fumbled through the pearls and rubies, then closed the box.

While these are priceless, she thought, they are not the *most* precious. Maybe my mother can help me.

Her mother, still mourning over her husband's death, opened her arms when Si-Ling entered the room. Embracing her daughter, she said joyfully, "Si-Ling, you have come back safely."

"I have one more riddle to solve before I can become empress," Si-Ling told her.

"Oh, my daughter, I cannot part with you. You are as precious to me as my own life. If you fail in your quest, my heart will break." A tear spilled from her mother's eye and slipped down her cheek.

Gently, Si-Ling wiped the tear with her own silk handkerchief, then folded it into her robe.

"Just one more meeting with the dragon," she promised, "and I shall come home to stay—and rule our empire."

The next day, Si-Ling appeared before the cave of the dragon. The creature was waiting for her, flames darting from its mouth.

"What priceless gem have you brought me?" the dragon roared.

Si-Ling bowed graciously. Then she opened her silk handkerchief.

"It is empty!" exclaimed the dragon.

"The most precious things are often visible only to the heart," Si-Ling answered. "My handkerchief holds the most precious jewel of all—a tear from my mother's eye."

For a moment, the dragon was silent, and smoke rose from its ears and nostrils. Then it spoke. "Ah yes, this is indeed the most precious of all gems. You have shown courage and wisdom, but most importantly, you have shown a heart of love. Go and rule in peace, Si-Ling."

Then the dragon, who was an honorable dragon, slithered back into its cave, and the trembling mountain was still once more.

When Si-Ling returned to the palace, her mother and the court officials welcomed her.

"Si-Ling has proved that the soul of wisdom is found in the heart of a child," said the wise mandarin.

And this is how Si-Ling became an empress who ruled her people well—with courage, wisdom, and love—in the land where mornings begin.

Skivvy and Cuttle

by Joan Lennon

I was teaching the stableboy to juggle eggs. He wasn't doing badly, either!

"Relax your shoulders," I told him. "Don't watch the eggs—don't watch anything! Good jugglers are in a world of their own. Now see if you can walk toward me without dropping anything."

I was juggling, too, you understand, so when we started to move, I was walking backward. I couldn't possibly have known that Glod, the Sheriff of Nottingham's bodyguard, would come into the kitchen just then. I couldn't have guessed he'd be stupid enough to stand right behind me. I could have told him that if he left his great feet there, I was bound to trip over them, and *then* I was bound to lose control of the eggs. Obvious, really.

But when I saw the expression on his face, with egg dripping down it, I realized this was not a time to chat. I picked up my skirts and ran. Not *quite* fast enough, but the bruise will heal. It's just a question of staying out of his way for a while. Like maybe the rest of my life.

My name is Skivvy, because that's what I do. I'm the maid-of-all-work in the Sheriff's kitchen, and if there's a dirty job or a bad-tempered kick going, it goes to me. That's it, and all of it, but to stop myself getting dreary, I try to learn new things as I go along. Like juggling—I learned that from some tumblers who were here last year. I've been practicing ever since.

I know all the best hiding places in the castle, and on this day I went right to the roof, up among the gargoyles and the pigeon droppings.

It was a hot, still day. I leaned on the parapet and gazed idly out across the great, green forest. It was nice up here, except for some flies that wouldn't leave me be. They seemed to be trying to bite the stone gargoyles, too, which I thought served them right, the bloodthirsty little pests. I watched one persistent fly buzzing round a little dragon-shaped gargoyle. *Buzz, buzz.* Horrible thing! Finally it settled on the gargoyle's nose, and you could tell it was thinking, I'm going to bite and bite—

Which was when I saw the gargoyle's tongue shoot out, catch the fly, and disappear again. There was the tiniest *crunch* and then—perfect stillness.

I couldn't believe my eyes. But . . .

"I saw you do that," I said. I didn't seriously expect an answer. And for a second, nothing happened.

Then the gargoyle's eye moved.

Not much. It was just a flicker—a quick glance, no more.

"I saw that, too!" I shrilled.

"Did not," said a muffled voice.

Pause.

"What did you say?" I whispered.

"I said, 'Did not.'" He sounded the way you do when you try to talk without moving your lips.

"I did, though," I said as firmly as I could. "I saw you move."

Another pause. Then the eye swiveled back again.

"Really?" said the voice.

"Really," I said.

And then the gargoyle just *sagged!* What had been a stiff, stone statue of a small dragon became . . . a *real*, small dragon. He draped himself along the warm stone of the parapet, and his eyes looked pleadingly up into mine.

"Please don't tell," he said.

My knees gave way. I flopped down beside him.

"Who would I tell?" I finally said with a shrug.

The dragon smiled, displaying impressively sharp, little, white teeth. Then he yawned and stretched, for all the world like a long, skinny cat. I reached out a hand to rub him under the chin. Cats like that.

I only just got my face out of the way in time.

"Oops—sorry. That's a ticklish bit," apologized the dragon as the smoke cleared.

I stared at the scorch marks along the stone and gulped. Little but lethal! He had a sweet smile, though. I grinned feebly back.

"I've been here since I hatched," the dragon continued. "Mama doesn't see very well, and she thought this was a cliff. I'll be joining her when my wings are strong enough. So far they're only good for little swoops."

"I wish I could leave," I sighed. "But it's no good going if you've noplace to go. I'd love to see you swoop, though."

The dragon started to speak, but I stopped him suddenly.

"Sh! Listen! Sounds like someone's being brought in."

We peered cautiously over the parapet. It was a long way down to the courtyard. But I had no difficulty identifying Glod, especially when he hit the prisoner across the face.

I could hear his sneering voice. "Take the King of

the Outlaws away. He can be King of the Dungeons—until we hang him tomorrow!"

"Oh no," I breathed. "Not Robin Hood!" I stood up.

"Don't go! Who? Take me, too!" chittered the dragon as he swooped about my head.

"No—you'll be seen—" I hadn't time for this.

"Not me!" crowed the dragon, and before I could stop him, he'd wrapped himself round my waist.

Great, I thought, *no one* will notice I'm wearing a dragon.

But when I looked down . . . no dragon. Just a bit of hemp with a funny buckle shaped like a dragon's head.

The buckle winked. "By the way, my name's Cuttle," he said. "Let's go!"

Down in the kitchen, everyone was whispering about the prisoner. The servants were all on Robin's side—nobody had any love for the Sheriff. But what could we do? Well, I thought, letting the other outlaws know what had happened to their leader was a start! I grabbed a basket and headed for the main gate.

"Gathering mushrooms. For the Sheriff's feast," I babbled at the guards, hoping they wouldn't stop to question me. But they were too busy gossiping, and I reached the trees without hindrance.

"So how do we find these outlaws?" came a voice at buckle level.

"We don't," I said, walking quickly. "They find us."

And before we had gone much farther, they did. A vision in red leaped out onto the path—red hat, red cloak, red boots, the lot—followed by a group of others who were more normally dressed.

"Hold, little maid," the vision in red said. "If you seek Robin's elusive band of Merrie Men, seek no more."

"Well, *you're* not hard to spot, for one!" I replied. "And I'm not little."

"See?" somebody said. "I told you it wasn't smart letting Will go around dressed like that."

"Look, Ben," said the vision. "I *have* to wear red. My name's Will *Scarlet*, right? It's not Will Green or Will Muddy Brown or—"

"There's something you need to know about Robin Hood," I said loudly.

The squabbling stopped abruptly.

"He's in the Sheriff's dungeon," I said.

There was a gasp of dismay.

"We've got to rescue him!"

"We've got to get him out!"

"You can't get him out without the keys," I said. "And the Sheriff holds those. You'd need to get very close to get them. Very close indeed . . . ," I added thoughtfully.

"What is it, girl?" said the one called Ben. "Have you got a plan?"

I nodded. "The beginnings of one," I said. "But I'd need a disguise—no, a costume. Something showy . . ."

All eyes moved from me to Will Scarlet.

"He's taller than she is, of course," murmured one of the Merrie Men.

"Not a problem," said Ben. "I can work miracles with a needle."

Will looked anxious. "What's going on?" he quavered. "Why are you all staring at me like that?"

"Don't worry, my deary," said Ben as he pushed Will back behind some bushes. "It's all in a good cause."

"Your Honor!"

Ben had been as good as his boast. He *had* worked miracles.

I stood before the Sheriff's guests looking as different from Skivvy the serving maid as scissors and needle could manage. My hair was cropped like a boy's, and Will's scarlet finery had been altered to my size. His cloak swirled from my shoulders, and round my waist I wore Cuttle as a glittering golden belt. No one would recognize me!

I hoped.

I made my bow. "Your Honor!" I said again. "My magic awaits your pleasure!"

There was a rustle of anxious whispers from the guests. What would the Sheriff's pleasure be?

"A magician?" he snarled, and I felt the blood drain away from my face. Then his mood changed, faster than a river eel, and he half laughed, half sneered, "Why not? Magician, *amuse* me."

Trying hard to ignore the threat in his voice, I bowed again and began.

"My lords and ladies," I intoned, "observe how the magic of the East molds matter and alters reality. Take a belt—"

With a flourish I brought Cuttle away from my waist. He unfurled with a satisfying *snap!* (only *I* heard the tiny "ouch!") and then, as I threw him into the air, he curled into a golden ball and landed on my hand.

"A ball." I held him up. "Or is it a flagon?" Cuttle rearranged himself. "Or a silver chain?" Cuttle drooped across my hands. "Or no, a ball after all." And adding two ordinary balls from under my cloak, I began to juggle.

The Sheriff was watching. So far, so good. But Glod, standing beside the Sheriff's chair, had me worried. He was staring at *me*, not my tricks. I had the horrible feeling he thought he knew me—and if he managed to make the connection between my face and those eggs, I was in *big* trouble.

Sweat was dripping down my back. I could feel my shoulders hunching and my neck beginning to ache. I knew I was going to drop something—spoil everything. And then, through my panic, I heard a sound.

It was rough, warm, and gravelly.

It was Cuttle. He was purring, from sheer excitement, I guessed, and it was as if somebody were singing in my ear, "You can do it! *We* can do it!"

I took heart.

"Hay—UP!" I cried as I abandoned the ordinary balls and threw Cuttle high, high into the air.

He uncurled with a squeal of delight and opened his wings. We had tied fire-red streamers to them, and he looked like a miniature phoenix swooping above the banqueters' heads. He was irresistible!

It was my chance.

I threw myself across the High Table and sliced the thong attaching the keys to the Sheriff's belt. Grabbing them as they fell, I swirled Will's cloak up, up, and over Glod. Before he could untangle himself, I clouted him, hard, with a heavy jug. He went down in a satisfying heap.

As I jumped back onto the floor, Cuttle let out a battle scream and dove at the Sheriff. Half the guests clapped and laughed, thinking this a part of the show. The other half were trying to push themselves away from the tables. For an instant, I thought the Sheriff was going to do nothing, but then I saw his eyes go slitty and his hand move from under the table.

I saw the knife.

There was no time to warn Cuttle. The Sheriff would have him in shreds before I could make the dragon understand the danger. So I didn't try. Instead, I leaped up as high as I could and caught Cuttle by the tail.

He came out of the air backward with a squawk.

Still holding his tail and supporting his chest with my other hand, I swirled him round to face the Sheriff.

"Drop the knife, sir!" I cried. "This dragon is loaded, and I'm not afraid to use him."

And to make sure he knew I meant it, I tickled Cuttle under the chin. The gush of flame that came out of his nostrils burned the food on the table to a crisp and singed the Sheriff's eyebrows.

His knife hit the floor, just as the great wooden doors of the hall crashed open behind me. I could hear people pounding in. For a moment I had no idea if they were friend or foe.

Then I heard Ben's big, welcome voice bellowing, "Hold it right there, my dearies! Nobody move!"

At first, nobody did. The rest was my fault. I got excited, you understand, and I must have tightened my grip. It's amazing how quickly tapestries catch fire. But I think it was the way the flame first blasted past his ear that made the Sheriff faint. He didn't hurt himself, though.

He landed on Glod.

In the forest, Robin Hood thanked us all for rescuing him and invited Cuttle and me to stay on with the Merrie Men. We were happy, and the Men were happy. (Except when Cuttle pointed his nostrils at them. They tended to leap sideways when this happened.)

But Will Scarlet *wasn't* happy. He stood there, dressed in borrowed green, looking at the sooty, torn remains of his finery. Even the cloak was beyond repair.

"I'm really sorry, Will," I said.

Will sighed.

But then Ben came forward. "I was able to keep some cloth back when I did the alterations," he said. "I made you these. And we all would like to think of you wearing them, Will Scarlet, my deary!"

From behind his back, Ben brought out a seriously scarlet garment.

Red . . . underpants!

The Fourth Question

A Chinese Legend
Retold by Vida Chu

*L*ong ago in China, there lived a young farmer named KaiWei. Every morning before the sun peeked over the horizon, he went to work in the fields. Too poor to afford oxen, he pulled his own plow, and bending like the willow tree, he planted rice seedlings one by one. He worked till the heavy black curtain dropped down from the sky and the stars twinkled like fireflies. Then, tired and covered with sweat and mud, he stumbled home. A handful of rice and a few stalks of bok choy were all he could give his mother for their supper.

The hut they shared was as threadbare as the tunic on his back. When it rained, KaiWei set out bowls and buckets to catch the water that poured through the roof. And when the north wind whistled, he covered the cracks in the walls with old rice sacks.

One morning KaiWei woke his mother and said, "I have made up my mind. I want to travel to the west to ask Buddha why, even though I work so hard, I am still so poor. I know he will help me."

His mother sighed. "The journey is long and dangerous, my son. But if your mind is made up, I will give you my blessing. Take care of yourself and come home soon."

KaiWei hugged his mother, and again she wished him a safe journey. He walked westward for eighty-one days. The sun was fierce, and his feet began to hurt.

When he came to a small cottage, an old woman offered him some tea.

"That is very kind of you," said KaiWei, and he walked in.

"Where are you going?" the woman asked.

"I'm going to see Buddha," KaiWei answered. "I want to ask him why, even though I work so hard, I am still so poor."

"Could you please ask Buddha why my daughter cannot speak?" begged the old woman.

"I'll be happy to," KaiWei promised, and he bowed and thanked her.

He walked for another eighty-one days. Rain poured like waterfalls out of the sky. KaiWei was cold and dripping wet when he walked into an orchard.

"Come in and have some tea with me," offered an old man.

"That is very kind of you," said KaiWei.

"Where are you going?" the old man asked.

"I'm going to see Buddha," KaiWei answered. "I want to ask him why, even though I work so hard, I am still so poor."

"Could you please ask Buddha why my orchard cannot bear fruit?" begged the old man.

"I'll be happy to," KaiWei promised.

After KaiWei left the old man, he walked for another eighty-one days. Leaves fell, and the sky turned cold and gray before he came to a great chasm. Roaring white water somersaulted between its steep cliffs.

KaiWei sighed as he stared at the river. Suddenly, the sky turned black. Wind howled. Thunder clapped. Lightning revealed an enormous dragon rising out of the water, a glowing pearl in the middle of its forehead. KaiWei trembled at the sight of this strange beast.

"Where are you going?" roared the mighty dragon.

"I am going to see Buddha," KaiWei answered. "I want to ask him why, even though I work so hard, I am still so poor. But now I am stuck. I cannot cross."

"That's easy!" said the dragon. "I'll carry you across.

But you must ask Buddha why, after wallowing in this muddy water for a thousand years, I have not risen to heaven."

"I'll be happy to," KaiWei promised.

The dragon arched its back, and KaiWei climbed on. He closed his eyes and hugged the dragon's slimy, scaly neck as, like a gust of wind, they whipped across the water.

When they reached the opposite shore, KaiWei gladly hopped off and bowed and thanked the dragon. Then he walked westward for another eighty-one days. Flowers bloomed, birds sang, and the bright sun smiled in the sky. He came to a hill, and on it stood a magnificent pagoda. "I feel in my heart that this is where I will find Buddha," KaiWei said, and he ran to the temple's entrance.

"Why are you here?" asked a guard at the gate.

"I've walked for a year," KaiWei pleaded. "Please let me see Buddha."

The guard led him to a great hall, and there sat Buddha.

"I know you have four questions to ask me," Buddha said to KaiWei, "but I'll answer only three. Choose carefully and ask."

KaiWei sighed. He yearned to ask his own question, but he could not disappoint those who had been kind to him. He decided to keep his promises and asked about the maiden who could not speak, the orchard that would not grow fruit, and the dragon who had not ascended to heaven.

Buddha whispered the answers in KaiWei's ear, and KaiWei bowed and thanked him. But he left with a heavy heart. His own question remained unasked.

After eighty-one days of sweating under the hot sun, he reached the chasm. The impatient dragon roared. "What did Buddha say?"

"Buddha said the pearl must be removed from your head," KaiWei replied.

"I've had this pearl for a thousand years," sighed the dragon. "Let me keep it for a few minutes more. You may take it off after the ride."

KaiWei climbed onto the slimy, scaly neck. With one swish of its tail, the dragon carried him across the great water. When KaiWei jumped onto the land, he stood on tiptoe to reach the dragon's forehead and remove the pearl.

Immediately, wings sprouted on each side of the dragon. Like a tornado it twisted out of the water and spiraled up to heaven.

"Keep the pearl," boomed the dragon as it disappeared into the clouds.

KaiWei put the pearl in his pocket and bowed to thank the dragon.

After eighty-one days, when the leaves turned fiery red and golden yellow, he came to the house of the old man.

"Buddha said you must dig in the orchard and unearth nine chests of gold and nine chests of silver," KaiWei told the old man. "Remove them and you will see a spring. Use its water on your trees."

The old man fetched two shovels. He and KaiWei dug deep into the soil and found the chests of silver and gold. When they dragged them out, water gushed up from the ground. Quickly they filled great wooden buckets and sprinkled the water carefully on the roots of the old man's trees. As if by magic, bunches of bright red litchi appeared on each bough. The happy old man gave KaiWei a basket of litchi, a sack of gold, and a sack of silver for his help.

The next day, with the basket of litchi in his hand, the pearl in his pocket, and sacks of gold and silver over his shoulders, KaiWei continued his walk home. After eighty-one days, shivering and blinded by snow, he came to the old woman's cottage. She welcomed him into her warm house.

"Buddha said when your daughter sees the one she loves, she will speak," KaiWei told her as he sipped a cup of hot tea.

Just then the daughter entered the room. She was surprised to see the young farmer and she opened her mouth and asked, "Ma, who is this handsome young man?"

The astonished woman, hearing her daughter's

voice for the very first time, was filled with joy. "MeiLing, do you like this young man?" the woman whispered.

"Like him?" her daughter said. "I wish I could marry him."

"Would you take my daughter to be your bride?" the woman asked KaiWei.

"I will be deeply honored," KaiWei replied, for he, too, had fallen in love.

The woman prepared a banquet and invited all her neighbors to the wedding. That night, fireworks decorated the sky while music and feasting filled the house.

The next morning, with the pearl in his pocket, the sacks of gold and silver over his shoulders, and his new bride by his side, KaiWei journeyed home. After eighty-one days, when tender green leaves appeared on the trees, and colorful butterflies fluttered among the wildflowers, they arrived.

"Ma, I am safely home," KaiWei called. "Come and meet my bride. I have so many things to show you."

While he was gone, KaiWei's mother had waited and worried. She had cried so much that her eyes were blind. KaiWei introduced his wife, but his mother could only touch her soft, young face. He placed the sacks of gold and silver in front of her, but she could only feel the coins and hear the clinking of the metal. With tears in his eyes, KaiWei pressed the pearl into his mother's hands and cried, "All my good fortune means nothing if my mother cannot see!"

Instantly the sparkle returned to his mother's eyes, for the pearl was magical. For the first time, she saw beautiful MeiLing, the sacks of silver and gold, and the magic pearl. But she was most happy to see her beloved son once again.

KaiWei continued to work hard, but now he was happy and content. When he grew old, he often sat in his courtyard, surrounded by grandchildren. He told them many stories, but their favorite was the one about their grandfather's journey to see Buddha and the fourth question that he never asked.

Nothing at All

by Julia Pferdehirt

The Eastern Kingdom stretched ten days' ride along the seacoast. Traders followed dusty roads from village to village, leaving kitchen knives or plow blades and taking away a winter's lacework, bags of spun wool, or great kegs of cider. The laws were few and fair, and the land was good. From harvest to harvest, all those who lived between the western mountains and the sea paid their taxes, held holiday each year on the king's name day, and generally kept the peace.

65

In a small village near the foothills there lived a remarkable family. The oldest child could run with such speed that people called him Seena, which means "The Antelope Runs." The second child was a story weaver who told tales of great wit and beauty. Everyone called her Ista, "The Sun Laughs."

When the third, and last, child was born, the villagers waited to see what her gift might be. Some thought she would become a great healer; others suggested a famous sculptor or a wise counselor to the king.

Years passed as this girl-child grew. She was gentle, kind, fun-loving, and clever. She made friends easily and would have been a joy to any parent's heart—except that she did nothing extraordinary. Her hands had no special skill, and her mind was no keener nor her judgment clearer than other people's. When her parents saw nothing unique in their daughter, they were shocked, and as time passed, the people in the village began calling her Ona, which means "Nothing at All."

During the autumn when Ona turned sixteen, the villagers heard rumbling in the western mountains. Sometimes the rumbling became a great roar that echoed across the valley. The oldest woman in the village said then that a dragon was on the rampage, but no one believed her, of course.

Nor did anyone believe her when the forest on the western mountains burned red for most of a week. Only when the streams from the western hills flowed with steaming water, and the mountain villagers fled with their bundles and their fear, did the people finally believe.

The villagers asked Ona's brother, Seena, to run to the king for help. Ona's sister, Ista, composed the message, pleading for the ruler to take the villagers under his protection. Scarcely had Seena disappeared on the eastern road than the people began gathering their possessions together. The roaring in the west told them that they, too, would soon be refugees, fleeing the dragon.

As the villagers prepared to leave, Ona wandered through the streets asking the old people what they knew about dragons. They knew very little. The oldest woman told her that dragons loved few things in the world besides gold, cruelty, and riddling.

"My mother once told me that dragons are magical creatures," the old woman said, "and that they riddle because they are cruel. But if you defeat them, they must give you whatever you ask for. My mother didn't say why, and I don't even know if it's true."

A neighbor told a similar tale about a dragon that lost its magic because it could not guess a riddle. Other than that, the villagers knew nothing. They were terrified.

That night Ona cried out as dragon shapes filled her sleep. She woke shaking and rose to look out the window at the western mountains. If the dragon pursues me even in my dreams, she thought, how will running away do any good? We have children and grandparents to slow us, and nothing at all to hold the dragon back.

With those words, "nothing at all," Ona nearly stopped breathing. She gripped the edge of the window sill and stared like a sleepwalker into the darkness outside. "Hold it back," she whispered to herself. "Nothing at all to hold it back." It was almost dawn when the foolish, impossible idea came to her.

Before sunrise, the people began their sad journey to the east, their rattling carts and bleating sheep raising clouds of dust. Ona took her basket and blanket and walked west toward the meadow. In the panic, she was not missed.

Ona spread her blanket on the ground in the very center of the meadow and sat facing the mountains. Throughout the afternoon she sat, small and unmoving. Toward evening she unwrapped some of the soft round buns her mother had made for the eastern journey. Tears dropped onto the napkin as she ate.

When the sun reached the crest of the western mountains, Ona saw the dragon dark against it. She saw its great wingspan and its long, reaching neck. The beast began its flight toward the meadow, and as it approached, Ona could see its claws and the black smoke curling from its nostrils.

The dragon landed with surprising grace in front of

her, but Ona did not move. When the dragon spoke, its voice was low, hoarse, and rumbling.

"You are a small one to be so foolish. Why did you not flee like the others?"

Its eyes narrowed, and cruel smoke rose slowly from its snout. Ona watched as its tail swept the ground only inches from her blanket.

"Speak!" said the dragon. "Amuse me, or I shall destroy you."

Now Ona spoke the words she had so carefully planned. "I have heard," she said slowly, "that you are a great riddler, and I could not imagine such a thing. I have come to see if it is true." She forced herself to look directly into the dragon's fierce eyes.

Perhaps the beast was amused. It stood silent for so long that Ona began to feel the coldness of the ground through the blanket. She heard the dragon's breath, low and grating. It was a terrible sound, a sound of waiting and trapping and great claws toying with helpless prey. She held her body still by sheer force of will.

It was almost a relief when the dragon finally spoke. "You?" it roared. "You? Fool, give me one reason why I should not flame you to ashes!"

Again Ona's dark eyes lifted to the dragon's great burning ones and held them. She heard herself say, "Because then you will never know the riddle. And I shall never know if you can answer it."

The dragon's tail swept great arcs across the ground, scraping the meadow raw, clear through the dark topsoil to the rock below. The grating sound of its breathing became a rumble as dark smoke poured from its nostrils. Suddenly, terribly, the beast bellowed and leaped into the air, all wings and hot breath. Ona closed her eyes, telling herself she would only be the first to die.

"Very well!" shouted the dragon. "Tell me this riddle of yours, and we shall see. But hurry; I do not waste my time with fools."

Now, for the first time, Ona moved. She stood up and faced the dragon. Behind the great creature, she could see smoke from mountain villages, charred to smoldering sticks by the dragon's flame. She had no real hope that her own home and crops would be spared, but she was determined to gain precious minutes for those who were running to safety.

"Listen carefully, dragon," she said loudly. "I will only say the riddle once. No true riddler needs to hear it a second time."

The dark smoke from the dragon's nostrils gave way to flame that singed the blanket. The girl smelled burned wool, but refused to lower her eyes. I play this game for all or nothing, she thought.

Speaking in a firm voice, she said, "Here is the riddle. . . .

"Nothing can defeat you, yet it may,
to gain the moment, to bar the way,
in silence and stone, in dark and in day.
One clue I will give you, no more I will say;
you must seek and find nothing to win this play."

The girl turned her back to the beast, drew the blanket around her head and shoulders, and sat down.

For nearly an hour, the two shapes huddled in silence. Then the dragon began to mutter to itself and shuffle back and forth like a prisoner pacing a cell. Ona ate some bread and drank from a water bottle. Although she did not turn her head, she could hear the dragon's words becoming louder and louder behind her.

"What game is this?" it rumbled. "Nothing can defeat me! Nothing! Do you hear, human?" Looking at the girl's turned back only magnified the dragon's growing rage. It stomped, raising billows of dust and raking its great tail over the stony ground.

Near sunset Ona could hear the dragon repeating bits of her riddle. For an hour it whispered the words "to gain the moment" over and over. She felt the creature's hot breath on her back as the sun slipped below the mountains and the gray skies dwindled to blackness. Then she sat, wrapped in her blanket, waiting for the sunrise. She hoped to be alive to see it.

During the coldest hour of the night, a howl slapped

the girl from her half-sleep. The dragon was roaring and shrieking, lashing its tail and crying out in frustration and rage. "Tell me, human," it screamed, "how am I to seek nothing? If this is a lie, I will show you no mercy!" This last the beast whispered with half-closed eyes, the smoke from its nostrils seeping out and sinking to the ground like a horrid creeping thing.

Ona thought she might scream from pure terror. She gripped the blanket about her with both hands and closed her eyes so she could not see the flames as the dragon flew in circles above her. Even when the heat beat against her face and the fire singed her hair, she did not move. Only as dawn approached and the dragon

flew toward the shadow of the mountains did Ona open her eyes to watch its fiery trail.

The beast did not return.

Sunrise was cold. Ona huddled on the hard earth and trembled. A clinging fog crept up from the foothills, turning the valley into a bowl of rolling gray smoke. Straining her eyes, Ona searched from north to south and back again, waiting for the shadow that would mark the dragon's return. She was terrified the beast might come without her seeing. Although she had no weapon, she did not want to be caught unawares. She pushed away the thought that she might scream and run mad with fear into the hills.

When the dragon did come, Ona was surprised by the silence of its flight. The creature circled three, then four times over the small, still figure on the ground. At last, folding its wings like great fans, the dragon settled in the open meadow in front of her.

"Human," the beast whispered, its voice scraping in Ona's ears like claws. Ona raised her eyes. The dragon continued to speak, low and harsh. "Did you know about the magic when you came?"

Ona was not about to give any answer that would allow the dragon to trick her, so she simply nodded.

"Then you expected to die, human," growled the dragon. "You knew that if I answered your riddle, you would lose and I would flame you to ashes." Tendrils of dark smoke crawled from its nostrils as the dragon began the slow pacing back and forth that Ona had seen during the night.

The dragon paced; Ona trembled. Neither of them spoke.

The silence continued. Ona had stopped wondering if she would die, when the dragon hissed, "Tell me the answer, human. Or do you have no magic to lose?"

"What do you mean?" Ona asked, her voice cracking. Her mind was working frantically to figure out what the creature was saying. Suddenly she recalled the neighbor's tale about the dragon that lost its magic. If only she knew more!

"Do not play with me!" screamed the beast. "You

spoke the riddle, and I have not answered it. Yet I do not hear you give the cry of victory and I do not hear the answer to this riddle from your own mouth. You have defeated me and yet you say nothing! What do you want?"

At that moment she knew the old people's confused snatches of memory had been true. The dragon did not know the answer. She had riddled and won, against all hope or possibility! And now . . . yes, what now? Evidently the dragon expected her to say or do something.

Ona rose, dropping the blanket behind her. When she spoke, her voice was firm. "Dragon," she said, "I did speak the riddle to you and I have not heard your answer. I am nothing, yet I have defeated you." Ona's voice grew louder as she spoke:

> *"Nothing can defeat you, yet it may,*
> *to gain the moment, to bar the way,*
> *in silence and stone, in dark and in day.*
> *One clue I will give you, no more I will say;*
> *you must seek and find nothing to win this play."*

Ona waited, watching the dragon closely. In a moment its eyes flashed and its brow raised, as if in surprise.

"That is correct, dragon," Ona said. "It is I who am Nothing, and it is I who have defeated you. I kept you here to gain time for my people as they ran from your evil greed. I barred the way in silence and stone. Consider, dragon, whether you saw me move or heard my voice in day or night. You did not!"

Now the joy of unexpected, even impossible, victory filled her. Ona cried up at the dragon, "I am Ona! Ona means Nothing at All! I am Nothing, and you did not find me!"

Now the dragon spoke so low, Ona could scarcely hear. "I see it is so. I have been defeated. What do you want? If I do not grant your wish, the magic of my flame will die."

"Go," commanded Ona. "Fly to the caves on the peak of the ancient mountains where no humans will ever build huts or plant gardens. If you ever return, dragon, or if one human dies under your flame, your magic will die. Go and never come back!"

The dragon raised its head and howled its fury and impotence and despair. Then the beast bowed its great, scaly head and said, "You have spoken, human. I will go. Still, your people are fools to call you Ona. Among my kind you would be called Kima, Kima Reetana."

The dragon spread its wings and flamed out of sight over the western mountains, leaving Ona to gather her things and return to the village.

Some days later Seena returned to the village as well. When the people had not seen smoke from their burning homes, they had sent their swiftest runner to investigate. He could hardly believe what he found.

Seena raced back to his family and friends on the muddy banks of the river to the east. He ran without stopping, swift as the antelope, to bring the news. "Ona was waiting for me," he panted. "The dragon has gone." The word "gone" formed in each mind and was whispered, passed like a precious stone from hand to hand. "Ona riddled with the dragon and won!" Seena continued. "She made the dragon leave."

The people collected their belongings and children and headed home. Along the road Ista the story weaver repeated the tale of Ona's riddle and the dragon's defeat. Each person passed the story on to the next, telling how Ona had sat in the meadow without moving or speaking to win time for the villagers' escape. The people could not walk quickly enough to satisfy their desire to see Ona, and to see the impossible miracle of their homes and crops still standing.

The celebration when the villagers returned was like the name days of ten kings! Ista was asked to tell the tale over and over, until the moon rose full and the grandmothers nodded over the sleeping children in their laps. Men and women alike held Ona's hands in theirs and wept. They were alive, and she had done a thing beyond the most amazing story!

From that time, the village celebrated Ona's victory

each year. The holiday was called Bar-reet, meaning
"The Great Riddle." Each year Ista, the story weaver,
told the tale of Ona and the dragon to the assembled
villagers, and each year the king sent a gift in Ona's
honor. And always her name was spoken with joy and
respect. Only she was no longer called Ona. Now all the
kingdom knew her as Kima Reetana—"Brave One,
Who Riddles with Dragons."

The Three Riddles

A Ukrainian Tale
Retold by
Eric A. Kimmel

Once there were three soldiers: a piper, a drummer, and a musketeer. One day they found themselves on a battle-field with bullets whizzing around their heads like bees.

"What are we to do?" said the piper. "We will surely be killed if we stay here."

"But if we run from battle, we will be hanged as cowards," said the drummer.

"There is a wheat field on the other side of that hill," said the musketeer, the most sensible of the three. "We can hide there until we think of what to do."

The three soldiers ran to the wheat field and hid themselves among the tall stalks of grain. As they lay there, they suddenly heard the sound of wings flapping overhead. A great dragon with gold scales landed in the field.

"What have we here?" the dragon said. "Three soldiers, I see. Shouldn't you be fighting in the battle that is raging on the other side of the hill?"

The piper and the drummer were too terrified to speak, but the musketeer addressed the dragon boldly, saying, "My friends and I have had our fill of war. Go ahead and devour us. We would rather end our lives quickly in a dragon's jaws than be shot to pieces on a battlefield."

"Indeed!" the dragon exclaimed. "I like your spirit. If you are as clever as you are brave, you may yet save your lives and make your fortunes."

"How so?" the drummer asked.

"I will carry you far away to a safe place where neither the enemy nor your officers can find you. I will provide for all your needs for the next seven years."

"What must we do in return?" the piper asked.

"Nothing very difficult," the dragon said. "I will tell you three riddles. At the end of seven years, I will ask you to answer them. If you can, I will trouble you no more. But if you can't, then you are mine to do with as I please. Do you accept?"

The piper, the drummer, and the musketeer huddled together to consider the dragon's offer.

"What kind of riddles will he ask?" the piper wanted to know. "I was never much good at riddles."

"They're probably very hard," the drummer said with a sigh. "We won't have a chance at guessing them."

The musketeer shook his head. "Can't you recognize good fortune when it stares us in the face? What have we to lose? If we stay in this field, we will die of hunger. If we attempt to leave, we will be killed by the enemy or hanged as deserters. The dragon is offering us seven years of life. A lot may happen in seven years. All of us may die. Or the dragon may die. Or we may discover the answers to the riddles. We have nothing to lose and everything to gain."

"We accept," the soldiers told the dragon.

The dragon carried them to a distant castle. He opened the gate with a golden key and led them through its hundred rooms, overflowing with treasure.

"This castle and everything in it belongs to you for the next seven years," the dragon said. "Should there be anything I have forgotten, I will give you this little whip. Crack it, and whatever you desire will appear."

The musketeer cracked the whip and said, "I wish I had a great feast." Instantly a table appeared, laden with cakes, pies, bread, roast meats, and flagons of wine. The soldiers sat down to eat and drink.

When they finished, the dragon said, "Now that your bellies are full, I will ask you the riddles. Listen closely. The first riddle is *What is our meat?* The second:

What is our spoon? And the third: *What is our wineglass?*
You have seven years to discover the answers." With
that, he spread his wings and flew away.

The piper and the drummer wasted no time in savoring
the castle's luxuries. There were closets of fine clothes,
chests of jewels, and servants to provide for every need.
Only the musketeer remained uneasy.

"What about the riddles?" he asked his companions.
"Shouldn't we be thinking of them?"

"What for?" the drummer and the piper replied. "We
haven't a hope of answering riddles like that. In seven
years the dragon will come for us, and that will be the
end. We may as well enjoy ourselves while we can."

But the musketeer was not prepared to give up so
easily. "The answers must be somewhere. I will go seek
them. If I am alive, I will return before the seven years
are up. If not, I bid you farewell until we meet again in
heaven."

The musketeer set out looking for the answers to the
dragon's riddles. He took the magic whip with him, and it
was a good thing he did, too, for whenever he needed a
pair of stout shoes, a warm cloak, or a purse full of coins,
he had only to crack the whip, and there it was. Thus he
traveled through the world for nearly seven years. At the
end of that time, he was no closer to solving the riddles
than the day he started.

One night the musketeer found himself high in the mountains. Snow began to fall, and he sought shelter in a cave. A long passageway led deep into the bowels of the mountain.

"I wish I had a light," he said. The musketeer cracked his whip, and a torch appeared. Holding the torch high, he followed the twisting tunnel. It led to a vast chamber where three dragons sat around a fire. A large piece of meat turned on a spit, its juices sizzling and hissing as they dripped onto the coals.

The musketeer extinguished his torch. He crept as close as he dared to hear what the dragons were saying.

"What is our meat?" the first dragon asked.

"The flesh of a sea cat from the far North Sea. That is our meat," the others replied.

"And what is our spoon?"

"The rib of a whale. That is our spoon."

"And our wineglass?"

"A drowned sailor's skull. That is our wineglass."

"So those are the answers!" the musketeer whispered to himself. He crawled back out of the cave and hurried down the mountain. As soon as he felt himself safe, he cracked the whip and said, "I want a horse with wings to carry me back to the castle." A winged horse appeared, and the musketeer leaped into the saddle. The horse flew into the air, leaving the dragon cave far behind.

*   *   *

Even on a winged horse, it took the musketeer a week to reach the castle. He arrived on the very day the seven years ended. He found his companions, the piper and the drummer, groaning with misery.

"Today we die! If only we had spent the seven years seeking answers to the dragon's riddles instead of wasting them on pleasure!"

"You are right," the musketeer said. The piper and the drummer looked up in surprise, for they'd believed him to be long dead. "Fortunately, my search was not in vain. I will share what I learned with you. When the dragon asks the first riddle, tell him . . ." He whispered the answer in the piper's ear. "And when he asks the second riddle, you must say . . ." He whispered the answer in the drummer's ear.

"And when he asks the third riddle?"

"Never fear. I know how to reply."

The musketeer had hardly spoken those words when they heard the sound of wings overhead. The dragon had come to claim his victims.

"Greetings!" the dragon said as he entered the castle. "I trust you have had a pleasant time here."

"We have, thanks to you," the musketeer answered.

"And now comes the time to pay for your lodging. Have you discovered the answers to my riddles?" He turned to the piper. "What is our meat?"

The piper answered, "The flesh of a sea cat from the far North Sea. That is our meat."

The dragon recoiled in surprise. "What is our spoon?" he blurted to the drummer.

"The rib of a whale. That is our spoon," the drummer said.

The dragon seethed with anger. "And what is our wineglass? Surely you cannot know that!"

The musketeer answered without hesitating. "A drowned sailor's skull. That is our wineglass."

The dragon snarled. "Someone told you the answers. You did not think of them yourselves."

"Fair or not, we have answered your riddles," said the musketeer. "Be off and trouble us no more!"

But the dragon would not be deprived of his dinner. He lunged at the three soldiers, breathing fire and smoke. The piper and the drummer cowered in a corner, but the musketeer boldly cracked his whip and said, "I wish we had a teakettle instead of this annoying beast."

At once the dragon turned into a bubbling samovar, a shining brass teakettle, that never went out and never went empty, no matter how many glasses of steaming tea the soldiers poured.

From that day on the piper, the drummer, and the musketeer were never again troubled by dragons and so lived happily ever after.

Sim Chung and the Dragon King

A Korean Folk Tale
Retold by Carol Farley

$\mathcal{L}$ong ago, people said that dragons lived in the waters surrounding the land of Korea.

"Dragons rule the bottom of the sea," fishermen told their sons. "Be careful that you do not upset our boat. If you fall into the ocean, you might be dragged off to the palace of the Dragon King, the fiercest, cruelest dragon of all!"

"Watch carefully when you go to fetch water," mothers told their daughters. "The water deep down inside the well flows out into the ocean. If you fall in, you could end up in the lair of the Dragon King!"

Even though she had no mother, Sim Chung heard this warning often because all the women of her village loved her. They admired her for her wit and beauty, but most of all they praised her for being a good daughter to her blind father, Sim Bang Sa. Her mother and brother had died, so now Sim Chung was the only one left to care for him.

Every day Sim Chung worked many hours in the homes and fields of a few wealthy landowners so that she could earn enough money for food and shelter.

"It isn't fair that you should have to work so hard!" Sim Bang Sa said one day. "If only I could see! I would gladly take care of you! But my eyes are as worthless as oil lanterns with no oil."

"Don't worry, *Aboji*," Sim Chung told him. "I can earn enough for both of us."

"But winter is coming soon," Sim Bang Sa said. "I'm worried, Jade Daughter. We should be buying many bags of rice to store away for the cold months ahead. You are just a child. How can you earn enough to keep us through the long, cruel winter?"

"I'll work even harder," Sim Chung answered. But no matter how hard or long she worked, she could not earn enough to buy extra food for winter. As the days grew shorter and colder, she was glad that her father could not see their empty rice boxes and bare vegetable bins. Sometimes she hardly had enough money for their daily food. On those days she would give her father everything and smack her lips and only pretend to eat.

Then a day came when she could earn no money at all, for snow covered the fields, and even the wealthy people stayed inside their homes. They sat on their warm floors and told her, "Come back in the spring."

"I am a disgrace," she told herself. "Aboji is depending on me, and I have failed." With great sorrow she walked to the ocean and wept. "Perhaps I should throw myself into the water," she whispered, "for I cannot bear to tell Aboji that we have no food left."

As she stood gazing out at the water, two sailors began talking nearby.

"Soon we must be off on our journey," one said. "We must find a maiden quickly, or the Dragon King will lash his tail so fiercely that our boat will sink into the sea and all of us will die."

"Yes," the other agreed. "If we throw a maiden into the waves, he will be appeased, and the water will become calm again. We have three hundred bags of rice for the family of the maiden who would come with us, but who would be brave enough to face the terrible Dragon King?"

Three hundred bags of rice! As she heard these words, Sim Chung caught her breath. If her father had such wealth, he could trade rice for vegetables and money and would be safe for many years to come.

Determined to be brave, she clenched her fists and marched up to the sailors. "I'll go with you."

The next day Sim Chung led the sailors, each carrying many bags of rice, into her father's home. Soon the little house was nearly bursting with the weight of all its new wealth.

"But how can this be?" Sim Bang Sa asked as he darted from one bag to another. He smiled and clapped his hands when he felt and smelled the contents. "Why has Buddha blessed us this way, dear daughter?"

Sim Chung had never lied to her father before, but she knew she could never tell him the truth, for he would never allow her to meet the fearsome Dragon King. "One of the wealthy families in the next village wishes to adopt me," she told him. "They have given you this rice in exchange for me."

Her father's smile vanished. "What? You'll no longer live here with me?"

"There's no need, Aboji. You no longer have to worry. Others will care for you now that you have so much wealth."

"Wealth?" Sim Bang Sa blinked his sightless eyes. "What good is wealth without love? You are far more precious to me than all the wealth in the world."

Sim Chung pressed the nails of her fingers deep into the flesh of her palms. She straightened her shoulders and tried to speak with a firm voice. "I think it is best for both of us that I do this, Aboji."

Her eyes were so filled with tears that she scarcely saw the pathway when she hurried out behind the sailors. As they walked toward the ocean shore, she heard them talking about what a brave, dutiful daughter she was, but her grief was so great she could take no pleasure in their words. Facing the Dragon King would be horrible, but never seeing her father again was the most terrible fate of all.

As soon as she reached the ship, she was brought before the captain. "Stay hidden in the room I have provided for you down below," he told her. "We will call you when we need you."

The dreaded call came only a few days later, for as the ship sailed eastward, the calm ocean suddenly became a raging whirlpool. Sim Chung knew that the Dragon King was commanding the gigantic waves and the howling winds. The sky darkened, the ship pitched, and anything that was not fastened securely to the deck went tumbling into the crashing, thundering water.

"It's the monstrous dragon!" screamed the sailors. "Fetch the girl!"

"I am truly sorry," the captain said as he helped Sim Chung struggle to the heaving deck. "But we have no choice."

The wet, salty wind whipped Sim Chung's clothing as she staggered to the rails of the lurching ship. She filled her lungs with one last breath of air, planted one last image of her dear father into her mind, and threw

herself into the raging sea. The icy water pulled her down, down in a cold spin. She clenched her eyes shut, then lost all thought as she sank in the swirling currents.

When she opened her eyes again, she was in a huge underwater palace looking at the mighty Dragon King himself. He was enormous—larger by far than she could have ever imagined. His scales were a brilliant green, and he had fierce red eyes. When he spoke, smoke poured from his mouth.

"I have caused the death of many who tried to cross over my kingdom," he raged as she bowed and trembled with fear. "I have known the thoughts and hearts of all." He drew closer and lowered his voice. "But I have never seen a child as unselfish as you, little Sim Chung."

Astonished, Sim Chung raised her head. "You know me?"

"I know all about you. You were willing to sacrifice your life so that your father would live. Because you have been such a dutiful daughter, I will not harm you. My home and wealth are yours. I have chests of pearls, rubies, and emeralds. What is it you desire?"

Sim Chung looked at the treasures surrounding her, but the jewels seemed dull and lifeless beside the glowing memory of her father. "Thank you for your kindness, Great Dragon King. But I desire only one thing. I wish to see my dear aboji once again."

"Then you shall!" said the Dragon King, and he

commanded a large lotus flower to open its petals. "Climb inside," he told Sim Chung, "and this flower shall rise to the surface of the sea. And I will give you this bag of pearls to take with you."

Safe inside the flower, Sim Chung rose up into the sunlight. As soon as the petals opened, she wrapped the bag of precious pearls around her waist and swam to the nearest shore. Exhausted, she fell into a deep sleep.

Hours later she was awakened by the cry of someone who had stumbled over her motionless body. She caught her breath in joyful wonder, for the voice was dearer to her than life itself.

"Aboji!" she shouted.

"Sim Chung!" The old man fell to his knees. "My daughter! Is it truly you? I've been searching everywhere for you! No one in the village knew where you had gone." So overjoyed was the old man that tears flooded his eyes and poured down his face.

The tears of joy that Sim Bang Sa shed suddenly washed away his blindness. "I can see!" he shouted. "At last I am able to see the precious face of my Jade Daughter!"

Sim Chung shed joyful tears, too. She and her father returned to their village, where for many years they lived in peace and contentment, ever thereafter singing the praises of the Dragon King.

The Shepherd Who Fought for a Princess

A Folk Tale from Poland

Retold by Gloria Skurzynski

When the world was young, Poland stretched green and golden from mountain to sea. In a castle on a hill above the River Vistula lived a good king with his beautiful daughter.

The king would have been happy except for one thing. A terrible dragon lived in a nearby cave, and each year, on the first day of spring, the dragon carried off the loveliest maiden in Poland.

No one knew how to kill the dragon. Its hide was

thicker and stronger than the building stones of the king's castle, and every one of its seven murderous heads could char a warrior where he stood. The dragon weighed so much that when it walked, the ground shook as if the earth were breaking apart. Its eyes glowed like flaming cinders, and its noses breathed foul, choking smoke.

The king knew that his daughter had grown to be the fairest maiden in Poland. Her hair was the color of ripe wheat, her eyes were as blue as the Polish sky, and her skin was as fresh as apricot blossoms. The dragon would surely carry her off when spring arrived once again.

"I cannot lose my daughter," the king cried. "Send forth a royal order. Every warrior in this land must try to kill the dragon. The one who slays it will win my daughter for his wife."

The first warrior to reach the castle was old and battle-scarred. His hair was streaked with gray, and even his armor looked gray with age. "I am still strong," he announced. "I have outlived three aging wives. Now I want a bride who is young and ripe."

The princess shuddered at the man's harsh words, but she hid her distress for her father's sake. "May your life be spared," she murmured bravely to the Gray Warrior.

When he left the castle, the Gray Warrior climbed above the dragon's cave, where he rolled huge boulders into a pile. With his bare hands, he broke off a tree and pushed the end under the pile of boulders.

"Come out, you great brute!" the Gray Warrior shouted to the dragon. "You have lived long enough."

The air before the cave blazed with blue smoke and red fire as the dragon appeared, its heads waving on seven long necks. The Gray Warrior leaned on the tree trunk to send boulders crashing down, but instead of harming the dragon, the rocks bounced off its hide like hailstones off a roof.

Raising its heads, the dragon breathed flame—and nothing remained of the old warrior but a pile of gray ashes.

The next contender to approach the king was young and haughty, with golden hair and bronze armor that glittered in the sunlight. "I will slay the dragon," the young man announced, "and then marry your daughter. And after I marry her, you must make me king." The young man's eyes gleamed with greed as he appraised the jewels on the royal crown.

With a sigh the king nodded. He was willing to give up his kingdom to save his daughter.

The princess could see that the Golden Warrior cared nothing for her but only wanted wealth and power. Yet she whispered, "May good fortune go with you, sir."

From the castle the young man went to a nearby woodland. There he chopped trees to build a wall of logs, leaving a hole in the middle. After he had coated the out-side of the wall with yellow clay, he mounted the barricade on wheels and thrust a long spear through the hole.

The Golden Warrior pushed the heavy wall before him along the path to the dragon's cave. "Come out, dragon!" he cried. "After I pierce your heart with my spear, I will be king!"

The dragon stretched forth its seven ugly heads. With only three of them it breathed—not very hard— on the young man, and in an instant the long spear was burned, the log wall turned to embers, and the Golden Warrior disappeared so that nothing remained of him but a pool of melted bronze.

Next came a laughing young warrior dressed in blue. "Life is a game," he said. "Love is a game. War is a game. If I kill the dragon, I will win the game, but if not, what does it matter?"

The princess had no desire to wed so foolish a man, but she wished him well as he danced out of the castle with heedless steps.

The dragon did not even bother to breathe on the Blue Warrior. With the tip of its tail, it flicked him far into the sky, and the Blue Warrior never returned to earth.

Other men tried to slay the dragon during the dismal winter months. The dragon dispatched so many of them that the king lost hope the beast would ever be slain.

Then, on a day so warm that ice melted in the Vistula River, a young shepherd arrived at the castle. "Sire," he said, "my name is Krakus, and I want to fight the dragon."

"The strongest warriors in my kingdom have tried to kill the dragon," the king said. "All have failed. And you, a shepherd lad, want to challenge it? You don't even wear armor."

"Still, I'd like to try," Krakus said.

"Throw your life away if you wish," the king muttered dejectedly.

The princess had been gazing at Krakus. He was so youthful and courageous that her heart went out to him. "Don't go," she begged. "The dragon will surely kill you."

"It's nearly spring, my lady," Krakus answered. "If I don't go, the dragon will carry you off. I won't mind losing my life in the hope of saving yours."

"May your brave heart beat for another hundred years, Krakus," the princess said as she tied her silk scarf around his wrist. Her eyes followed him with longing when he left the castle.

Instead of going to the dragon's cave, Krakus climbed the hill where his flock of sheep grazed. He threw wood onto the fire beneath an iron cauldron filled with pitch, until the pitch bubbled. Then he spread a fresh ram's skin on the ground.

Placing the cauldron of boiling pitch on the ram skin, Krakus sewed the skin around it. He hoisted the burden to his shoulder and made his way to the dragon's cave, treading softly to make no sound.

After Krakus had placed the pitch-filled skin in front of the cave, he waved the princess's scarf to attract the dragon's attention. "Come out and fight, you lazy, cowardly beast!" he shouted.

The dragon opened one of its fourteen eyes and snorted in contempt when it saw Krakus. The smoke made Krakus choke and cough, but he wiped his eyes with the princess's scarf and shouted again, "Are you too frightened to fight a stout-hearted Pole? I'll tie your seven heads into one great knot."

The dragon snorted again, in anger. Heat from the snort singed Krakus's hair, but he held his ground and cried, "I'll pluck the claws from your big, clumsy feet!"

The dragon grew furious, roaring blue-hot flames. Even though Krakus crouched behind a rock, the heat made him gasp for breath. He staggered to his feet, crying, "So you won't fight, you timid lizard! I'll feed your liver to my sheepdog."

Krakus broke into a run as the dragon burst forth from its cave. The beast knew that it could destroy Krakus with hardly any effort, so when it saw what looked like a fat ram lying in its path, it took a moment to devour the tidbit.

All the snorting and flame-breathing and raging anger had made the dragon very hot indeed, and after the ram skin reached the dragon's stomach, the pitch boiled furiously, scalding the beast's innards. The dragon slid to a halt, roaring with pain and surprise, then turned toward the River Vistula and began to drink with all seven heads.

It drank until the river lowered and fish found themselves on dry banks. Still seared inside, the dragon gulped more of the river. It drank until its hide stretched to seven times its size, and still the dragon drank. At last it swelled so much that it exploded. A great spray of water rose over the countryside and then poured down like a cloudburst, dropping pieces of dragon hide as big as building blocks.

Exhausted and scorched, Krakus made his way back to the castle, where the princess's tears of happiness washed the smoke stains from his face. The king was so elated to have his daughter safe that he made Krakus prince, and the young couple were wed.

The Polish people were so happy to be rid of the dragon that they built a large earthen mound in honor of Krakus. To this very day, that mound rises in the city of Cracow, Poland, which was named after the shepherd who killed the dragon.

The Black Dragon Princess

by Hildi Kang

The year Shining Pearl turned nine, nothing happened the way she thought it should.

In the eighth moon of Kyeh Hae, the king of Korea sent out a royal decree commanding all noble families to register their unmarried daughters. He wanted to choose a girl to marry the nine-year-old crown prince. The girl must be beautiful, intelligent, and kind, for she would become the next queen of Korea.

"I'm glad I don't have to go to the palace," Shining

Pearl murmured as she watched Pong-nae, her favorite servant girl, chop cabbage for summer kimchi.

She looked at her father, who sat smoking his long pipe. He was only a poor government official, and Shining Pearl was sure the king would want a girl from a high-ranking family. But that's not the way it happened.

Father put down his pipe and stood up. "The night you were born, Shining Pearl, I had a dream," he said. "I saw a black dragon, shining and graceful. I did not understand, for the dragon is a sign of royalty. Now I dare not withhold your name." He put on his black horsehair hat and went out to register her.

On the First Selection Day, Shining Pearl prepared to join the other young maidens at the palace. "I will remember everything I see," she promised her servant girl, Pong-nae. "I'll tell you all about it tonight." She put on her long silk skirt, and tied and retied the single loop in the bow of her short jacket.

Late that night, when the nose-tickling wisps of candle smoke blended with the sweet smell of roasted chestnuts, Shining Pearl sat on the floor with her family.

"The court servants wore flowing robes and hats trimmed with peacock feathers," she said. "We followed behind them to the king's pavilion. Great cinnamon red pillars hold up the roofs. Rafters in the ceilings are all painted in *tan-chong* designs of red, green, orange, and

yellow. And the royal dragons are everywhere, Father, painted on the ceilings, cut into stones on the bridges.

"But, Mother, I didn't know how to act in the palace! Court Lady Sonhi noticed my clumsiness, and she stood by me to correct me. She told me when to bow and where to place my hands, whether to speak or keep quiet. I was so confused I couldn't even think. It is good to be home. I don't ever want to leave again!"

Shining Pearl fell asleep nestled in her mother's arms, sure that this had been her one and only chance to see inside the forbidden palace. But that's not the way it happened.

By morning, rumors blew over the stone wall with every breeze. Soon a message came from the palace commanding Shining Pearl to return for the Second Selection Day. During the ceremony the king himself, dressed in golden silk robes embroidered with more of the royal dragons, came out from behind his private screen and said, "We have gained a beautiful daughter-in-law."

The queen said, "Please stay for lunch."

All the little princesses gathered round and made a great fuss over their new sister.

And right then Shining Pearl's life began to change.

Four royal servants in flowing black robes helped her climb into the royal palanquin. They lifted the poles across their shoulders and carried her home.

When the servants entered her family's courtyard,

Father came to the palanquin, raised the curtain cover, and lifted Shining Pearl out. She tried to hug him, but he wore his red ceremonial robe and talked to her using the highest and most complicated language, the kind used to address the king.

Shining Pearl ran to her mother, but Mother was making four big bows all the way to the ground in front of the royal messenger.

Everything tumbled around in Shining Pearl's mind. "I feel like a criminal with noplace to hide. I don't want to leave my mother and father. My heart is melting inside me!" Frightened, she fled to her room and wept tears that would not stop.

From that day on, she was no longer just a daughter. She had become a royal princess. To prepare for life in the palace, the queen's messengers arrived with skirts and jackets of green brocade, pine-pollen yellow, lavender silk, and crimson satin.

"Perhaps," said Shining Pearl as the family gathered round to inspect the elegant dresses, "being a princess will not be too bad. I will just come home every day to visit." But that's not the way it happened.

Great-uncle Hong stroked his white beard and shook his head slowly. "The forbidden palace is exceedingly strict. Once you enter it, you have said farewell to your family."

"Then I will write to you every day!"

But Father said, "You will have friends in the palace, but you will also have enemies. When you get letters from us, keep them only in your memory. Write back to us in the margins, returning the letters morning and night of every day. We will wash the ink away. There must be no record."

When night fell, her aunts took her outside in the bright moonlight. "Look at your home for the last time," they said. The cold, bitter wind blew icicles into Shining Pearl's heart and froze the tears on her cheeks. No one could comfort her.

In the morning came the command, "We await your arrival at the palace."

Shining Pearl took her maid, Pong-nae, and together they moved into Bright Spring Hall. The new princess stood looking at the cinnamon red pillars that were now her pillars, and the ornaments of gold and jade that were now her ornaments. She pushed back the sliding paper doors and looked out on gardens with snow-covered shrubs and ponds of crystal-clear water.

Now that I am a princess, she thought, surely I can do whatever I please. But that's not the way it happened.

Shining Pearl asked servants to invite her family to visit. But Chief Court Lady Choe declared, "The laws of the kingdom allow your father to visit you only on the first and the fifteenth of each month, milady."

Over the walls of her pavilion, Shining Pearl caught

glimpses of Crown Prince Changhon, calm and reserved, practicing with his bow and arrow. She asked if she could meet him. "Not until your wedding day, milady."

In the morning Shining Pearl put on her everyday clothes and began to study her lessons. Chief Court Lady Choe snapped, "The laws of the kingdom require you to greet the queen at dawn every morning with great bows, gowned in full ceremonial dress, milady."

When dusk came and the lanterns were lighted, Shining Pearl prepared to sleep. But Chief Court Lady Choe ordered, "The laws of the kingdom do not allow you to sleep yet, milady. You must make evening bows to the three majesties, the king, the queen, and the queen mother."

"I cannot live this way," sobbed Shining Pearl, hugging Pong-nae. "Chief Court Lady Choe has no human feelings at all. I am constantly afraid. I cannot be at peace, even for a moment. There is noplace for my own feelings."

Shining Pearl thought she would never, ever get used to the strict life in the palace, but even that did not turn out the way she thought it would.

The days passed, and gradually she did grow accustomed to her new life. The other princesses begged her to join their games. The queen said that she knew how Shining Pearl felt because she herself had left her family to come to the palace. The queen mother comforted and cheered the young princess when she needed it most and soon became like a real grandmother to her. And faithful Pong-nae stayed always at her side.

One day a gift arrived at Bright Spring Hall. "Another eight-paneled screen, milady, to beautify the room and stop the cold drafts." Shining Pearl stood respectfully as the serving ladies carefully unfolded the screen. Her eyes grew round with surprise. "Pong-nae, come quickly! Look!"

Fold by fold, the screen opened. Fold by fold, a jet-black dragon twisted and arched his way across the panels, staring down at Shining Pearl with bulging eyes, noble and proud. His scales, sprinkled with flecks of gold thread, glowed like fire against his black body. The colors pulled at her memory.

"A dragon! Exactly like the one my father saw in his dream!" Shining Pearl stared long at the screen, thinking. A tear slid down her cheek. Suddenly she turned and threw herself against Pong-nae, and sobs shook her body. The servant girl held her tightly and waited.

In time the room grew quiet. The little princess wiped her face on Pong-nae's sleeve, then turned back to face the dragon.

"I have two families now, Pong-nae, one here in the palace and one outside. Every day this dragon will remind me of them both. I will do my best to bring honor to my father and my mother. I will marry Crown Prince Changhon and become the next queen of Korea."

* * *

Shining Pearl never did become queen; her husband, the crown prince, died before ascending the throne. However, both her son and her grandson grew up to become kings of Korea.

Born in 1735, Shining Pearl lived at a time when girls in Korea did not learn to read or write. The princess did learn, however, and when she was sixty years old, she wrote a book about her life in the palace. Although she is known to us only as Crown Princess Hong, she says in her story, "I was the second daughter in the family, and Mother and Father treasured their two little pearls."

The King's Dragon
by Jane Yolen

There once was a soldier who had fought long and hard for his king. He had been wounded in the war and sent home for a rest.

Hup and one. Hup and two. He marched down the long, dusty road, using a crutch.

He was a member of the Royal Dragoons. His red-and-gold uniform was dirty and torn. And in the air of the winter's day, his breath plumed out before him like a cloud.

Hup and one. Hup and two. Wounded or not, he marched with a proud step. For the Royal Dragoons are the finest soldiers in the land and—they always obey orders.

After a bit, the soldier came upon a small village. House after house nestled together in a line.

Just the place to stop for the night, thought the dragoon to himself. So he hupped and one, hupped and two, up to the door of the very first house. He blew the dust from his uniform, polished the medals on his chest with his sleeve till they clinked and clanked together and shone like small suns. Then he knocked on the door with his crutch.

Now, that very first house belonged to a widow, and she, poor woman, was slightly deaf. When she finally heard the sound of the knock, she called out in a timid voice, "Who is there?"

The soldier puffed out his chest. He struck his crutch smartly on the ground. "I am a Royal Dragoon," he said, "and I am tired and hungry and would like to come in."

The woman began to shake. "The royal *dragon?*" she cried, for she had not heard him clearly. "I did not know the king had one. But if it *is* a dragon, and hungry besides, I certainly do not want him here. For he will eat up all I have and me as well!" She so frightened herself that she threw her apron up over her head and called out, "*Go away!*" Then weeping and wailing, she ran out her back door to her neighbor's home.

The Royal Dragoon did not see her leave, of course. But as she had told him to go, go he did, for the Royal

Dragoons are the finest soldiers in the land and—they always obey orders.

Hup and one. Hup and two. He marched to the second house and knocked on the door. He stood at attention, his chest puffed out, and in the cold, wintry air, his breath plumed out before him like a cloud.

Now, that second house belonged to the widow's father, and he, poor man, was nearly blind. He listened to his daughter's story, and when the knock came, the two of them crept up to the window. She still had her apron up over her head, and he could see no farther than the end of his nose. They peered out, and all they saw was the great plume of breath coming from the soldier's mouth.

"See," said the daughter, "it *is* a dragon. And he is breathing smoke."

"Who is there?" called out the old man in a timid voice.

"I am a Royal Dragoon," said the soldier. As he spoke, even more clouds streamed from his mouth. "I am tired and hungry and would like to come in."

"*Go away!*" cried the old man. "No one is here." Then he and his daughter ran out the back way to their neighbor's house, weeping as they went.

The Royal Dragoon did not see them leave, of course. But as he had been told to go, go he did, for the Royal Dragoons are the finest soldiers in the land and— they always obey orders.

Hup and one. Hup and two. He marched to the third house and knocked on the door. He stood at attention, his chest puffed out, and saluted so smartly his medals clinked and clanked together.

Now, the third house belonged to the mayor, and a very smart young mayor he was. He could see perfectly well. He could hear perfectly well. And when the widow and her father finished their story, the mayor said, "The king's dragon, eh? And just listen to that! I hear his scales clinking and clanking together. He must be terribly hungry indeed and ready to pounce."

So the mayor called out the door, "*Wait, Sir Dragon.*" Then the mayor and the widow and the widow's father ran out the back. They gathered together all the other people in the town, and without even taking time to pick up their belongings, they ran and ran as fast as they could, until they came to the mountains, where a very real dragon lived. When it came out and ate them all up, not a one of them was surprised. They were already convinced of dragons, you see.

As for the Royal Dragoon, he stood waiting at attention in front of the third house for a very, very, very long time. He may be standing there still. For the Royal Dragoons are the finest soldiers in the land. And—they always obey orders.

Kotoshi the Dragon Doctor

by Phillis Gershator

It was the time of year, in a small Japanese village by the sea, to choose a maiden as a sacrifice to the local dragon.

The dragon lived in a cave in the sea cliffs. If the villagers did not offer it a maiden every year, it got angry and churned around violently in the sea. It thrashed its long, scaly tail this way and that until the waves rose so high that the shore flooded and the boats at sea capsized. So many people drowned in the floods and storms that sacrificing a single maiden seemed a small price to pay for the lives of all the other villagers and sailors.

The names of the maidens were written on separate slips of paper and placed in a barrel, and one slip was selected by a village elder. Kotoshi's name was chosen this year. Her parents wept, but what could they do?

"I will not go meekly," Kotoshi told them. "I will fight to defend myself. I will try to kill the dragon. Even if I fail, it will be better than doing nothing."

"If you attack the dragon and fail, it will go on a rampage. Then not only will we have lost you, but many others will also die in the dragon's storms and floods," her parents replied, fearing the worst.

"We have endured storms and floods even when other maidens went quietly to their deaths. The dragon is hateful and cruel. I must attempt to rid our village of this cursed creature. Don't forget," Kotoshi reminded her parents, "I am skilled with a knife."

Kotoshi was, in truth, skilled with a knife. She assisted her father when he doctored the villagers. From him she had learned how to lance an infected wound and remove warts, tumors, and moles from the body. She had also learned how to set broken bones and how to ease pain with herbal potions and massage. She knew good herbs from bad and she helped her father prepare medicines for fever and sickness of all kinds.

When the time for the sacrifice came, Kotoshi was brought in a carriage to the rocky seaside cliffs. Her family and friends followed the carriage, weeping and wailing. She waved a last farewell from the rocks and watched the people grow smaller and smaller as they slowly made their way back to the village.

Kotoshi settled down to wait for the dragon. In her sash she had hidden her knife. In her basket of food she carried medicines, in case she was wounded in battle and survived to doctor herself.

Hours later, there was still no sign of the dragon. Kotoshi crept down among the rocks, looking for shelter from the sun and wind. From a nearby cave echoed the sound of great, gulping sobs. Kotoshi crept closer to the cave's opening. In the dim light she saw a large dragon with a small one lying at its feet.

"I am Kotoshi," announced the maiden. "I was sent to save my village from your wrath."

"Not now, not now," cried the dragon. "My baby is dying!"

"What is the matter?" asked Kotoshi.

"I don't know. If it were a surface wound, I could heal it with my own blood, but something is eating away at my baby from inside."

"I have some knowledge of illness," Kotoshi said. "Maybe I can help, if you will allow me to examine the baby."

"If you can help me," the dragon said, sniffing, "I will let you return to your village. I never liked human flesh anyway. I only exacted sacrifices because they made everyone fear and respect me."

Kotoshi's examination revealed that the baby dragon

had broken its wing. The break had not healed properly, and the wing was swollen and infected.

"I will have to pierce the infected area to release the poisons trapped inside," she told the mother dragon. "Then the wound must be cleaned and the wing reset. We will need a bit of wood to use as a splint. I already have a knife and medicine and I can tie the splint with my sash."

Kotoshi put the baby dragon to sleep with some herbs so it wouldn't feel any pain; then she went to work while the mother dragon watched. When the baby awoke, Kotoshi gave it more medicine to bring down its fever. She cared for it all night and day, until finally, the fever broke.

"Your baby will be fine now," Kotoshi said. "I will come back in a few days to remove the splint."

"No, you cannot go," said the mother dragon. "How do I know you will return?"

"But I will starve here," protested Kotoshi.

"I will bring your food, the same food we eat: seaweed and fish."

Since the dragon wouldn't let her leave the cave, Kotoshi made the best of it. She talked to the dragon about life in the village and explained that the people were poor and dependent on the sea for their meager livelihood. She told the dragon that when huge waves rocked the ocean and storms blew up unexpectedly, everyone suffered and many villagers drowned.

The dragon told her that it was dragon nature to frolic in the water. Even a hundred sacrificial maidens couldn't keep dragons from swimming in the sea. Dragons did not intend to cause havoc, but of course, if they were angry or upset, they tended to thrash about.

"That is why the villagers offer you a maiden each year—to appease your anger," Kotoshi said.

"But I told you, I don't care for meat," complained the dragon. "I prefer fish. The villagers might as well leave me a basket of fresh fish."

"When I go home, I will tell that to the elders," Kotoshi promised.

"Make sure the fish are alive," said the dragon.

Once the baby's wing had healed, the dragon kept her word and allowed Kotoshi to return to the village. She also gave Kotoshi a precious gift.

"Since you saved my baby," the dragon said, "you may prick my tail and collect nine drops of blood. Everyone knows that dragon blood heals an open wound."

Kotoshi preserved the precious blood in one of her medicine jars. She thanked the dragon and promised that the villagers would reward her with offerings of live fish, now and in the future.

People could hardly believe the good news: Kotoshi had come back alive! Her parents saw her and wept, this time for joy. The elders listened carefully to her tale.

Henceforth, they announced, the villagers would offer live fish to the dragon. No maidens had to be sacrificed ever again. An offering took place that very week. Everyone trooped to the seaside cliffs, singing and dancing and carrying baskets of live fish for the dragon. How different from the mournful parade that had accompanied Kotoshi's sacrificial journey!

In time, life returned to normal. Kotoshi continued to help her father doctor the villagers. If a patient's wound would not heal, she used a drop of the precious dragon blood, and the wound healed instantly, as if by magic.

When she saved a life that would have been lost without the dragon blood, Kotoshi led a special procession to the cliffside cave. The villagers left mountains of fish there for the dragon and her baby. And to show their appreciation, the dragons played far, far out at sea so they wouldn't churn up the monster waves that so often ravaged the coast of Japan.

The Last of the Dragons

by E. Nesbit

Of course you know that dragons were once as common as buses are now, and almost as dangerous. But as every well-brought-up prince was expected to kill a dragon and rescue a princess, the dragons grew fewer and fewer, till it was often quite hard for a princess to find a dragon to be rescued from. And at last there were no more dragons in France and no more dragons in Germany, or Spain, or Italy, or Russia. There were some left in China, and are still, but they are cold and bronzy, and there never were any in America. But the last real live dragon left was in England, and that was a very long time ago, before what you call English history began. The dragon lived in Cornwall in the big caves amidst the rocks, and a very fine big dragon it was, quite seventy feet long from the tip of its fearful snout to the end of its terrible tail. It breathed fire and smoke, and rattled when it walked, because its scales were made of iron. Its wings were like half-umbrellas—or like bat's wings, only several thousand times bigger. Everyone was very frightened of it, and well they might be.

Now the King of Cornwall had one daughter, and when she was sixteen, of course, she would have to go and face the dragon. It would not eat her, of course—because a prince would come and rescue her. But the Princess could not help thinking it would be much pleasanter to have nothing to do with the dragon at all—not even be rescued from it.

"All the princes I know are such very silly little boys," she told her father. "Why must I be rescued by a prince?"

"It's always done, my dear," said the King, taking his crown off and putting it on the grass, for they were alone in the garden, and even kings must unbend sometimes.

"Father, darling," said the Princess presently, when she had made a daisy chain and put it on the King's head, where the crown ought to have been. "Father, darling, couldn't we tie up one of the silly little princes for the dragon to look at—and then I could go and kill the dragon and rescue the prince? I fence much better than any of the princes we know."

"What an unladylike idea!" said the King, and put his crown on again, for he saw the Prime Minister coming with a basket of new-laid bills for him to sign. "Dismiss the thought, my child. I rescued your mother from a dragon, and you don't want to set yourself up above her, I should hope?"

"But this is the *last* dragon. It is different from all other dragons."

"How?" asked the King.

"Because it *is* the last," said the Princess, and went off to her fencing lesson, with which she took great pains. She took great pains with all her lessons—for she could not give up the idea of fighting the dragon. She took such pains that she became the strongest and boldest and most skillful and most sensible princess in Europe. She had always been the prettiest and nicest.

And the days and years went on, till at last the day came that was the day before the Princess was to be rescued from the dragon. The Prince who was to do this deed of valor was a pale prince, with large eyes and a head full of mathematics and philosophy, but he had unfortunately neglected his fencing lessons. He was to stay the night at the palace, and there was a banquet.

After supper the Princess sent her pet parrot to the Prince with a note. It said:

"Please, Prince, come to the terrace. I want to talk to you without anybody else hearing.—The Princess."

So, of course, he went—and saw her gown of silver a long way off shining among the shadows of the trees like water in starlight. And when he came quite close to her he said, "Princess, at your service," and bent his cloth-of-gold-covered knee and put his hand on his cloth-of-gold-covered heart.

"Do you think," said the Princess earnestly, "that you will be able to kill the dragon?"

"I will kill the dragon," said the Prince firmly, "or perish in the attempt."

"It's no use your perishing," said the Princess.

"It's the least I can do," said the Prince.

"What I'm afraid of is that it'll be the most you can do," said the Princess.

"It's the only thing I can do," said he, "unless I kill the dragon."

"Why you should do anything for me is what I can't see," said she.

"But I want to," he said. "You must know that I love you better than anything in the world."

When he said that, he looked so kind that the Princess began to like him a little.

"Look here," she said, "no one else will go out

tomorrow. You know they tie me to a rock and leave me—and then everybody scurries home and puts up the shutters and keeps them shut till you ride through the town in triumph shouting that you've killed the dragon, and I ride on the horse behind you weeping for joy."

"I've heard that that is how it is done," said he.

"Well, do you love me well enough to come very quickly and set me free—and we'll fight the dragon together?"

"It wouldn't be safe for you."

"Much safer for both of us for me to be free, with a sword in my hand, than tied up and helpless. *Do* agree."

He could refuse her nothing. So he agreed. And next day everything happened as she had said.

When he had cut the cords that tied her to the rocks, they stood on the lonely mountainside looking at each other.

"It seems to me," said the Prince, "that this ceremony could have been arranged without the dragon."

"Yes," said the Princess, "but since it has been arranged with the dragon—"

"It seems such a pity to kill the dragon—the last in the world," said the Prince.

"Well, then, let's not," said the Princess. "Let's tame it not to eat princesses but to eat out of their hands. They say everything can be tamed by kindness."

"Taming by kindness means giving them things to eat," said the Prince. "Have you got anything to eat?"

She hadn't, but the Prince owned that he had a few biscuits. "Breakfast was so very early," said he, "and I thought you might have felt faint after the fight."

"How clever," said the Princess, and they took a biscuit in each hand. And they looked here and they looked there, but never a dragon could they see.

"But here's its trail," said the Prince, and pointed to where the rock was scarred and scratched so that it made a track leading to the mouth of a dark cave. "Look, that's where it's dragged its brass tail and planted its steel claws."

"Let's not think how hard its tail and its claws are," said the Princess, "or I shall begin to be frightened—and I know you can't tame anything, even by kindness, if you're frightened of it. Come on. Now or never."

She caught the Prince's hand in hers, and they ran along the path toward the dark mouth of the cave. But they did not run into it. It really was so very *dark*.

So they stood outside, and the Prince shouted, "What ho! Dragon there! What ho within!" And from the cave they heard an answering voice and great clattering and creaking. It sounded as though a rather large cotton mill were stretching itself and waking up out of its sleep.

The Prince and the Princess trembled, but they stood firm.

"Dragon—I say, dragon!" said the Princess. "Do come out and talk to us. We've brought you a present."

"Oh, yes—I know your presents," growled the dragon

in a huge rumbling voice. "One of those precious princesses, I suppose? And I've got to come out and fight for her. Well, I tell you straight, I'm not going to do it. A fair fight I wouldn't say no to—a fair fight and no favor—but one of these put-up fights where you've got to lose— No. So I tell you. If I wanted a princess, I'd come and take her, in my own time—but I don't. What do you suppose I'd do with her, if I had her?"

"Eat her, wouldn't you?" said the Princess in a voice that trembled a little.

"Eat a fiddlestick end," said the dragon very rudely. "I wouldn't touch the horrid thing."

The Princess's voice grew firmer. "Do you like biscuits?" she asked.

"No," growled the dragon.

"Not the nice little expensive ones with sugar on the top?"

"*No,*" growled the dragon.

"Then what *do* you like?" asked the Prince.

"You go away and don't bother me," growled the dragon, and they could hear it turn over, and the clang and clatter of its turning echoed in the cave like the sound of steam hammers.

The Prince and Princess looked at each other. What *were* they to do? Of course it was no use going home and telling the King that the dragon didn't want princesses —he wouldn't believe it. And they could not go into the cave and kill the dragon. Indeed, unless it attacked the Princess it did not seem fair to kill it at all.

"It must like something," whispered the Princess, and she called out in a voice as sweet as honey and sugar-cane, "Dragon! Dragon dear!"

"WHAT?" shouted the dragon. "Say that again!" and they could hear the dragon coming toward them through the darkness of the cave. The Princess shivered, and said in a very small voice, "Dragon—dragon dear!"

And then the dragon came out. The Prince drew his sword, and the Princess drew hers—the beautiful silver-handled one that the Prince had brought in his motorcar. But they did not attack; they moved slowly back as the dragon came out, all the vast scaly length of it, and lay along the rock, its great wings half spread and its silvery sheen gleaming like diamonds in the sun. At last they could retreat no farther—the dark rock behind them stopped their way—and with their backs to the rock they stood swords in hand and waited.

The dragon drew nearer and nearer—and now they could see that it was not breathing fire and smoke as they had expected—it came crawling slowly toward them, wriggling a little as a puppy does when it wants to play and isn't quite sure whether you're cross with it.

And then they saw that great tears were rolling down its brazen cheeks.

"Whatever's the matter?" said the Prince.

"Nobody," sobbed the dragon, "ever called me 'dear' before!"

"Don't cry, dragon dear," said the Princess. "We'll call you 'dear' as often as you like. We want to tame you."

"I *am* tame," said the dragon. "That's just it. That's what nobody but you has ever found out. I'm so tame that I'd eat out of your hands."

"Eat what, dragon dear?" said the Princess. "Not biscuits?"

The dragon slowly shook its heavy head.

"Not biscuits?" said the Princess tenderly. "What, then, dragon dear?"

"Your kindness quite undragons me," it said. "No one has ever asked any of us what we like to eat—always offering us princesses and then rescuing them—and never once, 'What would you like to drink the King's health with?' Cruel hard I call it," and it wept again.

"But what *would* you like to drink our health with?" said the Prince. "We're going to be married today, aren't we, Princess?"

She said that she supposed so.

"What shall I take to drink your health with?" asked the dragon. "Ah, you're something like a gentleman, you are, sir. I don't mind if I do, sir. I'll be proud to drink your and your good lady's health with a tiny drop of"—its voice faltered—"to think of you asking me so friendly like," it said. "Yes, sir, just a tiny drop of gagagagagasoline—that—that's what does a dragon good, sir—"

"I've lots in the car," said the Prince, and was off down the mountain like a flash. He was a good judge of character, and he knew that with this dragon the Princess would be safe.

"If I might be so bold," said the dragon, "while the gentleman's away—p'raps just to pass the time you'd be so kind as to call me 'dear' again, and if you'd shake claws with a poor old dragon that's never been anybody's enemy but its own—well, the last of the dragons'll be the proudest dragon there's ever been since the first of them."

It held out an enormous paw, and the great steel hooks that were its claws closed over the Princess's hand so softly she hardly felt them.

And so the Prince and Princess went back to the palace in triumph, the dragon following them like a pet dog. And all through the wedding festivities no one drank more earnestly to the happiness of the bride and bridegroom than the Princess's pet dragon, whom she had at once named Fido.

And when the happy pair were settled in their own kingdom, Fido came to them and begged to be allowed to make itself useful. "There must be some little thing I can do," it said, rattling its wings and stretching its claws.

So the Prince had a special saddle made for it—very long it was—and one hundred and fifty seats were fitted to this, and the dragon, whose greatest pleasure was now to give pleasure to others, delighted in taking parties of children to the seaside. It flew through the air quite easily with its hundred and fifty little passengers, and would lie on the sand patiently waiting till they were ready to return. The children were very fond of it and used to call it "dear," a word that never failed to bring tears of affection and gratitude to its eyes. So it lived, useful and respected, till just the other day—when someone happened to say, in its hearing, that dragons were out of date, now so much new machinery had come. This so distressed the dragon that it asked the King to change it into something less old-fashioned, and the kindly monarch at once changed it into a modern machine. The dragon, indeed, became the first airplane.

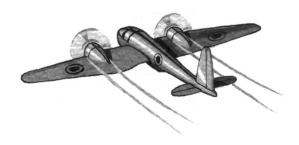

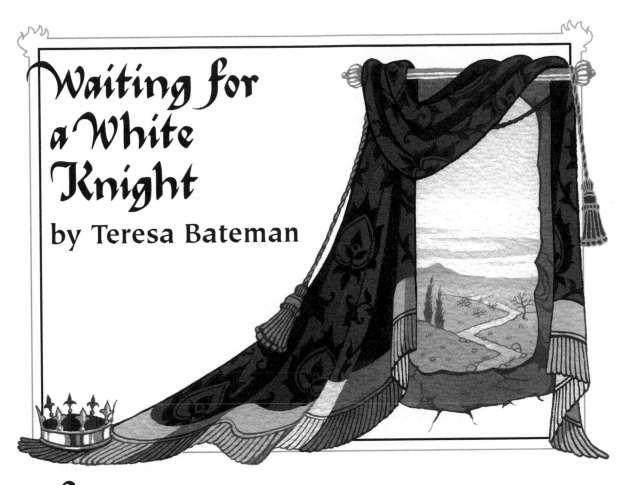

Waiting for a White Knight

by Teresa Bateman

Samantha looked longingly out the cave window and down the dirt road that wound to the mountain's foot. The road, as always, was empty. Few ventured along it, and those who did (and survived) quickly told others of its dangers. This made travelers even more infrequent.

Heaving a sigh, Samantha turned back into the cave. Her stomach rumbled, and she realized it was lunchtime.

Living in a cave wasn't bad, she thought. In fact, it

137

was very comfortable. Her family had been living there for years. A housing shortage in the kingdom had forced many to give up castles and resort to rock walls and roofs.

Each generation in Samantha's family had added touches and treasures that turned the cave into a lovely home, richly decorated and certainly worth a visit. Visitors, however, were rare, and Samantha was lonely. More than that, she was disappointed. All her young life she had been told that someday a white knight would come up that winding dirt road to her doorstep. He would be riding a noble steed and wielding a silver sword that glittered in the sunlight.

She had been promised this white knight by her mother, who had been promised the same by her mother before her. Samantha's mother had assured her that a white knight was worth waiting for. Her mother's eyes had grown dreamy as she'd recalled her own white knight so many years past.

Samantha had heard the tale a thousand times— how her mother's white knight had ridden boldly up the dirt road, calling her mother out of the cave by name (doubtless acquired through a local wizard). His voice had echoed through the caverns like a bell, and her mother, always somewhat shy, had advanced hesitantly. The knight had rushed forward to meet her. . . . Just thinking about it made Samantha long for her own white knight.

She sighed again. She had grown weary of waiting. Some days it felt as though he'd never come. It wasn't that she never met any men. Others had come through the years, but none had lived up to her expectations. It just wasn't fair!

She glanced out the window again, blinked, then stared. A small dust cloud had appeared at the base of the mountain. Someone was coming up the road.

She shivered in anticipation and leaned forward, straining to get a closer look at the traveler. As he drew nearer, she noticed the white steed with the shield hanging from its saddle, catching the light like a mirror.

"Could it be?" she asked herself eagerly, afraid to hope.

She could hear the jingling of harness now, the clinking of mail. He rounded the nearest bend, sword sparkling in the sunlight. He was so handsome—black hair brushing a noble brow, armor gleaming. And at that moment Samantha knew. She KNEW. This was *her* white knight.

He drew nearer and swung down off his horse, drawing his sword and advancing toward the cave entrance.

"Samantha!" he shouted. "I've come for you."

"I knew it, I knew it!" Samantha said, pausing for a moment to check her teeth and puff on a bit of perfume. "He's everything Mother said he'd be, and more."

She hurried along the tunnel and sprang from the cave door—surprising the knight, who fell backward.

She crisped him with one burst of flame and munched him down. Then she sighed.

"Mother was right," she muttered, using her talons to pick her teeth, then settling back on her haunches, wings curled neatly behind her. "Delicious! He *was* worth waiting for."

She sighed and gazed anxiously down the road.

"A pity that travelers are so infrequent," she muttered, taking wing and circling the mountain. "Now, where's that white horse?"

Author Biographies

Teresa Bateman grew up in Issaquah, Washington, as the second oldest of ten children. A graduate of Ricks College and Brigham Young University, she received her Masters in Library Science at the University of Washington. An avid traveler, Ms. Bateman has lived in Argentina, Honduras, and a remote community in bush Alaska called St. Marys. Her writing awards include the Anne Izard Storytellers' Choice Award and the Paul A. Witty Short Story Award, given annually by the International Reading Association. Among her many picture books are *The Ring of Truth*, *Farm Flu*, and *The Merbaby*. She is currently the librarian at Brigadoon Elementary School in Federal Way, Washington.

Vida Chu was born in Macao, grew up in Hong Kong, and came to America in 1960 to study biology at the University of Pennsylvania. In addition to retellings of Chinese folk tales in *Cricket*, she enjoys writing poetry, which has been published in the *Kelsey Review*, *Princeton Arts Review*, *US 1 Worksheet*, and *The Literary Review*. She recently returned from Yunnan, a southwest province of China, where the world's only living hieroglyphic language is still being used by the Naxi nationality. Ms. Chu and her husband live in New Jersey and have two children.

Carol Farley once lived in Korea, where she learned to love the stories Koreans told long ago. Two of them are featured in her picture books *Mr. Pak Buys a Story* and *The King's Secret*. Dragons are also important characters in many tales from ancient Korea and, like the dragon in "Sim Chung and the Dragon King," they often helped humans. In addition to stories about Korea, Ms. Farley has written mystery novels for young people. Most of these books take place in Michigan, where she now lives.

Phillis Gershator's books include picture books such as *Tiny and Bigman* and *When It Starts to Snow* and her chapter books *Someday Cyril* and *Sugar Cakes Cyril*. Her retelling of an African folk tale ZZZNG! ZZZNG! ZZZNG! won an Anne Izard Storytellers' Choice Award. Her stories and poems have also appeared in *Cricket*, *Spider*, and *Ladybug*. Ms. Gershator was a children's librarian with the Brooklyn Public Library before moving to the U.S. Virgin Islands, where she now lives on the sunny island of St. Thomas.

Joan Hiatt Harlow's award-winning stories are bits and pieces of who she is. Her mom was born in Newfoundland, and Ms. Harlow's childhood was filled with stories and songs about Newfoundland ("The Beautiful Rock") and the lovable, loyal Newfoundland dogs. It's no surprise that she grew up to write *Star in the Storm*, which takes place in 1912 Newfoundland. Her dad was a well-known Boston singer who told her exciting and mysterious stories, bits and pieces of which she adapted for her book *Joshua's Song*, which takes place in 1919 Boston during the "Great Molasses Flood." As an adult, she made an amazing visit to China, where dragons lurked everywhere—in statues, carvings, and decorations. They watched her wherever she went. Some were scary and some were wise. Her dragon in "Si-Ling and the Dragon" is bits and pieces of all the dragons she met in China.

Hildi Kang is an educator and writer with a special interest in Korea. Her writing includes articles about Korea and four books for teachers (one of which was awarded the *Earlychildhood NEWS 2000 Directors' Choice Award*). An active traveler, she often visits family in Korea, has hiked in Switzerland, biked in southern France, and explored the ancient trade routes of China and Uzbekistan. She lives with her husband in Livermore, California.

Eric A. Kimmel's grandparents came from the western Ukrainian town of Kolomyya, which is why many of his favorite books are set in Ukraine. These include the Caldecott Honor Book *Hershel and the Hanukkah Goblins* and *The Birds' Gift: A Ukrainian Easter Story*, which was a featured book at the 2001 Easter Egg Roll at the White House. Check out his Web site at www.ericakimmel.com.

Joan Lennon was born in Canada and lives in a village in Scotland with a husband, four tall sons, and two short cats. She is doing her best to gain a reputation as "World's Worst Juggler" in the schools she visits and can now make it all the way down a narrow hall on her unicycle by holding onto both walls and squealing. Her chapter book *There's a Kangaroo in My Soup!* was published by Cricket Books, and her play *Midas Goes for Gold* is performed by the traveling Kenspeckle Puppets at schools and festivals around Scotland.

Patricia MacLachlan has written picture books, novels, and screenplays. She was awarded the 1986 Newbery Medal for her book *Sarah, Plain and Tall*. She is currently working on three picture books with her daughter, Emily. The first, *Painting the Wind*, is due to be published in April 2003. She lives in western Massachusetts with her husband, two dogs, and one cranky cat.

Geraldine McCaughrean has written over 125 titles, from picture books to adult novels. She has been published in twenty-five countries and won a dozen major awards. For children, she writes novels and playlets, retells world myths, and has adapted such classics as *Moby Dick*, *El Cid*, and *The Pilgrim's Progress*. Her novel *The Kite Rider* concerns a boy who risks everything riding kites through the skies of thirteenth-century China. Her latest novel, *Stop the Train*, is set in Oklahoma in 1894. Both books were simultaneously shortlisted for the prestigious Carnegie Medal (the United Kingdom's equivalent of the Newbery Medal). Ms. McCaughrean lives in Berkshire, England, with her husband John, daughter Ailsa, and Daisy the dog.

E. (for Edith) Nesbit wrote almost a hundred books during her lifetime. Born in London in 1858, she produced such classics as *The Railway Children* and *Five Children and It*. When she died in 1924, a manuscript entitled "The Last of the Dragons" was found among her papers. It was published a year later and has remained popular with children ever since.

Julia Pferdehirt believed every one of her grandpa's wild, silly stories when she was a girl—even the ones about meeting talking rabbits and getting sticks in his stocking from Santa Claus. With such a grandfather, it's no wonder she became a writer and story-teller! *Cricket* magazine has a special place in Julia's heart because her very first story, and some others, too, were published there. Since then she's written stories and books, including *Freedom Train North: Stories of the Underground Railroad in Wisconsin* and *They Came to Wisconsin*, a collection of immigrants' stories. Ms. Pferdehirt also visits schools across Wisconsin telling true stories from history.

Gloria Skurzynski is the award-winning author of fifty children's books, including picture books, nonfiction science books, science fiction, historical novels, and mysteries. She and her husband, Ed, have five grown daughters and are the grandparents of four boys and three girls. Although Ms. Skurzynksi was born in Pittsburgh, Pennsylvania, she has lived in the West for half her life. Visit her Web site at www.gloriabooks.com to learn more about her.

Jane Yolen has loved dragons forever. She has certainly written a lot of books with dragons in them, from *Here There Be Dragons* and *Merlin & the Dragons* to The Pit Dragon trilogy and the Arthurian book *The Dragon's Boy*. Her picture book *Dove Isabeau* has a dragon in it, too. She has 230 other books, with fairies, unicorns, space-hopping toads, midnight walks to see owls under a shining moon, and all sorts of other wonders. She is a wife, a mother of three, a grandmother of four, and lives part-time in a farmhouse in Massachusetts and part-time in a stone mansion in Scotland. She loves to read, write, listen to music, watch movies, go antiquing, find lost castles, and one day hopes to see a real, live, actual dragon. You can find out more about her at www.janeyolen.com.

"The Three Riddles" by Eric A. Kimmel, © 2002 by Eric A. Kimmel
"Skivvy and Cuttle" by Joan Lennon, © 2002 by Joan Lennon
"Thoughts of a Drought Dragon" by Geraldine McCaughrean, © 2002 by Geraldine McCaughrean

Illustrations © 2002 by Nilesh Mistry
Compilation copyright © 2002 by Carus Publishing Company
All rights reserved
Printed in the United States of America
Designed by Ron McCutchan
First edition, 2002

Grateful acknowledgment is made to the following for permission to reprint the copyrighted material listed below.

Teresa Bateman for "The Dragon at the Well" from *Cricket* magazine, September 1994, Vol. 22, No. 1, and October 1994, Vol. 22, No. 2, © 1994 by Teresa Bateman, and for "Waiting for a White Knight" from *Cricket* magazine, October 1993, Vol. 21, No. 2, © 1993 by Teresa Bateman. Vida Chu for "The Fourth Question" from *Cricket* magazine, April 1999, Vol. 26, No. 8, © 1999 by Vida Chu. Curtis Brown, Ltd., for "Dragons: An Unnatural History" by Jane Yolen, © 2002 by Jane Yolen; for "Dragon's Coo" by Patricia MacLachlan, first published in *Cricket* magazine, January 1984, Vol. 11, No. 5, © 1983 by Patricia MacLachlan; and for "The King's Dragon" by Jane Yolen from *Here There Be Dragons*, published by Harcourt Brace & Co., © 1993 by Jane Yolen; first published in *Spaceships and Spells* by HarperCollins Publishers, © 1987 by Jane Yolen. Carol Farley for "Sim Chung and the Dragon King" from *Cricket* magazine, April 1999, Vol. 26, No. 8, © 1999 by Carol Farley. Phillis Gershator for "Kotoshi the Dragon Doctor" from *Cricket* magazine, January 1996, Vol. 23, No. 5, © 1996 by Phillis Gershator. Joan Hiatt Harlow for "Si-Ling and the Dragon" from *Cricket* magazine, September 2000, Vol. 28, No. 1, © 2000 by Joan Hiatt Harlow. Hildi Kang for "The Black Dragon Princess" from *Cricket* magazine, March 1996, Vol. 23, No. 7, © 1996 by Hildi Kang. Julia Pferdehirt for "Nothing at All" from *Cricket* magazine, March 1996, Vol. 23, No. 7, and April 1996, Vol. 23, No. 8, © 1996 by Julia Pferdehirt. Gloria Skurzynski for "The Shepherd Who Fought for a Princess" from *Cricket* magazine, December 1980, Vol. 8, No. 4, © 1980 by Gloria Skurzynski.

Library of Congress Cataloging-in-Publication Data

Fire and wings : dragon tales from East and West / edited by Marianne Carus.— 1st ed.
    p. cm.
Summary: A collection of stories about all kinds of dragons, by such authors as Jane Yolen, Patricia MacLachlan, Eric A. Kimmel, Vida Chu, and E. Nesbit.
  ISBN 0-8126-2664-8 (alk. paper)
  1. Dragons—Juvenile fiction. [1. Children's stories. 2. Dragons—Fiction.
3. Short stories.] I. Carus, Marianne. II. Mistry, Nilesh, ill.
  PZ5 .F467 2002
  [Fic]—dc21

                                                          2002005792

SOMALIA

A Crisis of Famine and War

Edward R. Ricciuti

THE MILLBROOK PRESS
Brookfield, Connecticut

Published by The Millbrook Press
2 Old New Milford Road
Brookfield, CT 06804
© 1993 Blackbirch Graphics, Inc.
5 4 3 2

Created and produced in association with Blackbirch Graphics.
Series Editor: Bruce S. Glassman

Library of Congress Cataloging-in-Publication Data

Ricciuti, Edward R.
    Somalia: a crisis of famine and war/Edward R. Ricciuti.
    Includes bibliographical references and index.
    Summary: Explores the crisis of famine and war in Somalia by tracing its
evolution through the nation's history and politics.
ISBN 1-56294-376-6 (lib. bdg.)
ISBN 1-56294-751-6 (pbk.)
    1. Somalia—Politics and government—1960–   —Juvenile literature.
2. Insurgency—Somalia—History—20th century—Juvenile literature. 3.
Famines—Somalia—History—20th century—Juvenile literature. 4. Food
relief—Somalia—History—20th century—Juvenile literature. [1. Somalia—Politics and government—1960–   . 2. Somalia—History—20th
century. 3. Famines—Somalia.] I. Title.
DT407.R53 1993
320.96773—dc20   93-15094
                                                           CIP
                                                           AC

Contents

4

Chapter 1

Barren Land, Warrior People

Minutes after midnight on December 9, 1992, camera lights drove back the darkness on an African beach. From the pitch-black sea, men in combat gear, faces and clothing camouflaged, waded ashore in the glare of the lights.

It looked as if a movie were being filmed, but that was not the case. This was a *real* landing. The men hitting the beach were U.S. marine scouts and navy SEALS (Sea-Air-Land Forces), who were heavily armed and ready for combat. Instead of confronting an enemy on the sands, however, they ran into a crowd of television-camera operators and journalists recording the landing.

Battle was not the objective of the landing party, nor of the thousands of troops who followed it, although all were ready to defend themselves. Their purpose was to save lives. Operation Restore Hope, an effort to feed millions of starving people in Somalia, was the mission they were there to accomplish.

Operation Restore Hope, covered by news media from all over the world, was a huge humanitarian effort undertaken by the combined military forces of many countries. Troops from around the globe risked their lives in an attempt to ensure that vital food and medicine reached the suffering people of Somalia.

Africa's eastern-most country has been battered by civil war, drought, and famine for several years.

Opposite:
Many Somalis are desert nomads who must remain constantly on the move in search of food and water. Unable to find either, these women wait in line for relief.

Starving Somalia

Somalia, the easternmost country in Africa, had been battered by civil war, drought, and political unrest for several years in the late 1980s and early 1990s. In January 1991, rebel groups united to topple the government of President Muhammad Siad Barre. Soon afterward, however, these groups started fighting among themselves. Without government, lawlessness swept the country. Gangs of gunmen looted and killed.

A U.S. Army transport plane and armored vehicles arrived at the airport in Mogadishu, Somalia's capital, on December 9, 1992. U.S. marines delivered the first shipments of military supplies needed to secure the city from armored gangs.

A Somali reaches out to a U.S. marine as he shows his delight at having a friendly military presence in the city of Mogadishu.

Riding around in trucks mounted with machine guns and grenade launches were rival gang members who loaded onto their vehicles food supplies stolen from relief convoys. Most of them were personally armed with automatic assault rifles, which they used to fight one another and to murder innocent civilians.

The combined effects of the drought and violence caused many Somalis to die and millions of others to flee the countryside. They flocked to the cities, the biggest of which is Mogadishu, Somalia's capital. Conditions there were nightmarish. Buildings were holed and battered by bullets and shells, electric power and sanitary facilities had failed, and there was almost no food or medicine.

The Red Cross and other relief organizations tried desperately to get food and medicine to the people but were powerless against the well-armed gangs. Gunmen killed relief workers and stole food that was meant for the hungry. As the situation grew worse, the United States, with the support of the United Nations, decided to take action. Thus, Operation Restore Hope was born.

Led by the United States, troops from many nations went into Somalia to protect relief workers and supplies for the stricken Somalis. Never before had such a huge military effort been launched to save lives. Together, world leaders had decided that only a military force could counter the activities of the gangs and their leaders.

Blood Ties

Some of the gangs were merely bandits, looting and killing at random. Most, however, were forces loyal to powerful leaders called warlords. Their loyalty was based on a centuries-old Somalian tradition of ancestral ties known as the clan system.

A clan is a large group of people who trace their descent to the same ancestors. Almost all Somalis think of themselves as clan members. In Somalia, there are a half-dozen major clans, plus several smaller ones, each divided into subclans. The largest clans have about 100,000 members each and dominate different parts of the country. Most Somalis are more loyal to their clan or subclan than to their nation.

In the past, clan members were governed by groups of elders. During the late 1980s and early 1990s, however, the warlords assumed power and leadership. Each of these men had his own territory, base of operations, and gangs to do his fighting.

Somalia at a Glance

Size: 246,000 square miles (slightly smaller than Texas).
Population: 6,709,000 (1991 estimate).
Land: Plateaus and plains, with rugged mountains in the north rising to almost 8,000 feet.
Climate: Hot; two wet seasons with about 11 inches of annual rainfall. Only two permanent rivers, both in the south. Frequent, long droughts.
Major Religion: Islam.
Capital: Mogadishu.

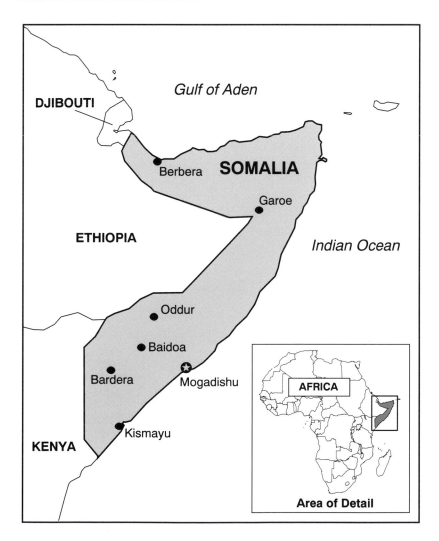

This map shows Somalia's surroundings and major cities. The inset locates it on the African continent.

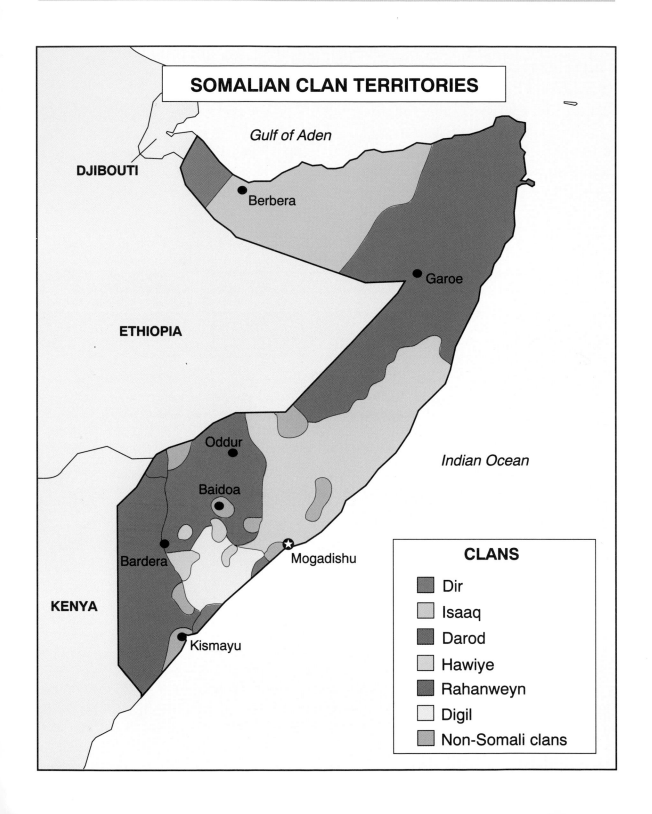

SOMALIAN CLAN TERRITORIES

Gulf of Aden

DJIBOUTI

Berbera

Garoe

ETHIOPIA

Oddur

Indian Ocean

Baidoa

Bardera

Mogadishu

KENYA

Kismayu

CLANS

- Dir
- Isaaq
- Darod
- Hawiye
- Rahanweyn
- Digil
- Non-Somali clans

Such internal division was not new in Somalia. Throughout Somalia's history, different clans have fought one another, frequently over land. Clan rivalry over territory continues right down to the present. This rivalry was responsible for the violence that swept Somalia and devastated its people.

Clan territories are those on which certain clans have been grazing and watering their livestock for centuries. Some clan territories overlap, and some extend into neighboring countries. Not all the land occupied by clans is under their direct control, especially outside Somalia.

There is a certain irony to the country's clan rivalry. Somalia is the only black African nation in which a single language, Somali, is spoken by almost everyone. It is also the only one inhabited by a single people (only a small number of non-Somalis live there). This ethnic uniformity gives the Somalis a strong sense of identity. Somalia has not experienced the ethnic warfare that occurs in many other African countries and elsewhere in the world, but its clan rivalries have been just as destructive.

A Warrior People

Clan rivalry in Somalia is rooted in the way of life of its people. Many Somalis are nomads, or wanderers. They travel in groups from place to place, seeking water and pasture for their herds of camels, cattle, sheep, and goats. Conflicts with one another over water and grazing rights have made many nomadic peoples around the world aggressive, and the Somalis are no exception.

The Somalis have always been fighters, with almost all men considered warriors. In fact, *warrior* is the term still used for an adult man. Aggressiveness and suspicion toward strangers are qualities admired in a Somalian male.

Somalian fighting men once carried shields, spears, swords, double-edged knives, and bows and arrows. Except for the knife, most of these weapons have been replaced by firearms, but the warlike attitude of the past remains and has contributed to the fighting in Somalia that led to starvation and suffering.

Land of Little Rain

Nearly a quarter of Somalia's land is desert and, of the remaining land, only a small portion is suitable for farming. Because drought and poor growing conditions plague the region, many Somalis struggle to survive with little food and water. Here, a nomadic family travels through the desert in search of water.

Water and pasture became crucial to the Somalian people because of the country's climate and geography. Somalia is located in the Horn of Africa in the northeastern part of the continent and is bordered by the countries of Djibouti, Ethiopia, and Kenya. About one fourth of Somalia is desert; there are also mountains and plateaus and dry, grassy plains dotted with bushes and low trees.

Only a few areas are suitable for farming, so most people rely on livestock for survival.

The Somalis fight a constant battle against drought, which makes it difficult for farmers to stabilize the food supply. Most of the year, there is no rain. There are two seasons in which rain generally falls—March to May and September to December, but often rain does not even come at these times. During drought, famine is common. Even in good times, most Somalis have just enough food. Year after year, moreover, their country ranks among the world's poorest. Consequently, control of the resources that support livestock has meant nothing less than survival for the Somalis since their beginning as a people.

Somalian Origins

Somalis have lived in the Horn of Africa for perhaps a thousand years. Scientists are not sure where they lived before that, however. Most Somalis claim descent from the Arab tribe called the Quraysh, which is the tribe of the Prophet Muhammad, who founded the religion of Islam.

Whether or not they descended from the Arabs, which most scholars dispute, Somalis have been greatly influenced by the Arabs. Most Somalis have Arab blood, and Arabic is one of the country's two official languages.

More than a thousand years ago, Arabs established towns on the coast of Somalia. After the Somalis moved into the region, many Arabs intermarried with them, and the Somalis eventually adopted the Sunni branch of Islam, the religion of the Arabs.

Many Somalis live in parts of the bordering countries of Kenya and Ethiopia, occupying a fifth of Kenya and a quarter of Ethiopia. Somalis in these three countries think of themselves as one nation, even though international borders separate them. This nationalism, referred to as pan-Somalism, has caused conflict between Somalia and its neighbors for hundreds of years.

Modern Somalia Emerges

Until the nineteenth century, the land populated by the Somalis was divided into city-states and territories ruled by clans. During the last half of the nineteenth century, all that changed. Great Britain, Italy, France, and Ethiopia sought influence in Somalian territories. The Europeans established trading centers and gradually expanded their control in what is today Somalia, while Ethiopia grabbed a chunk of Somalian land called the Ogaden.

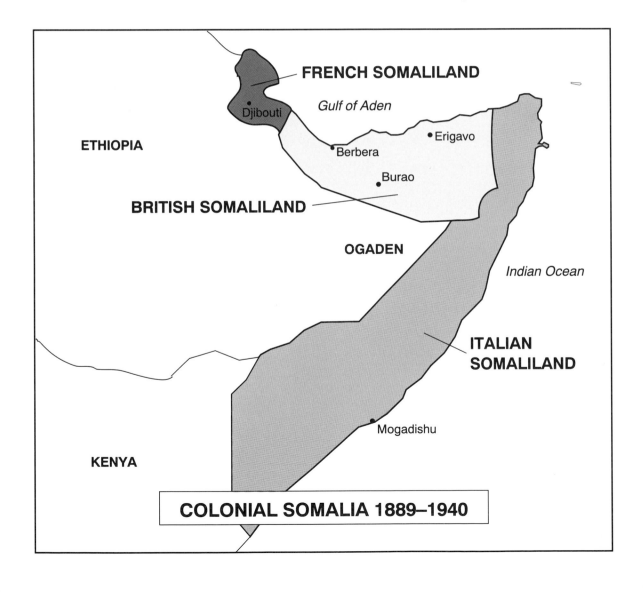

COLONIAL SOMALIA 1889–1940

During this period of colonization, the region was plagued by conflicts and tensions among rival European powers. The majority of the conflicts were border disputes and disagreements over trading interests. One dispute, the Fashoda Incident of 1898, brought the region to the brink of war. The conflict centered around Great Britain's actions to link Egypt with South Africa by rail. To do this, the railway was threatening to cut into an important French trading route that ran across Africa from Senegal to Somaliland. In an effort to stop Britain, the French sent a military party to meet the British. Although war appeared certain, diplomatic negotiations prevented a full-scale battle.

By the early 1900s, Britain had a foothold in northern Somalia (British Somaliland), and Italy controlled the southern area (Italian Somaliland). The French held what is now the tiny nation of Djibouti. There was little resistance by Somalis to colonial rule, although during the 1940s an independence movement took shape.

During World War II, the British drove Italian forces from the region, but in 1949 the United Nations agreed to let Italy administer Italian Somaliland in order to prepare the country for independence in 1960. Meanwhile, the colonial government in British Somaliland began to guide its Somalian territory toward independence. During this time, Somalis formed political parties, held local elections, and assumed positions in the government. On July 1, 1960, Italian Somaliland and British Somaliland became the independent Somali Republic. The Ogaden, however, which Somalis claimed, remained in the hands of Ethiopia, to whom the British had given it in 1948.

Independence did not bring about much positive change to Somalia on any front—economic, political, social, educational. Chronic drought, a lack of modern agricultural techniques, refugee problems, civil war, war with Ethiopia, and a corrupt and inefficient government have all contributed to Somalia's lack of development.

Chapter 2

From Independence to Revolution

T he first president of the independent Somali Republic was a long-time political leader, Aden Abdullah Osman. From the start, he ruled a troubled nation. Different clans had joined with opposing political parties, increasing existing rivalries. Moreover, the government was unstable and in time grew corrupt.

Most political parties, however, supported the government policy, backing the Somalian rebels in Ethiopia's Ogaden. In 1964, a brief but vicious border war erupted between Somalia and Ethiopia. Meanwhile, Somalia tried to claim the area of northeasten Kenya, which was inhabited by people of Somalian blood. Somalia's government armed rebels in Kenya to fight Kenyan security forces. Between 1963 and 1967, two thousand of these rebels were killed by the Kenyans.

Revolution

In July 1967, a progressive politician named Abdirashid Ali Shermarke, a member of the powerful Darod clan, was elected president. He tried to eliminate corruption and conflict and bring opposing clans together, and his prime minister was able to smooth relations with Ethiopia and

Somalia has struggled to find political allies in order to survive.

Opposite:
Siad Barre took control of Somalia in 1969, after the assassination of Abdirashid Ali Shermarke, the country's president. Here, Siad Barre (left) meets with King Baudouin of Belgium in 1978, during a tour of Europe.

Two Ethiopian soldiers lie waiting on the Somalia-Ethiopia border during the war between the two countries in 1964.

Kenya. Then on October 15, 1969, disaster struck. Shermarke was shot and killed by a police officer who felt his clan group had been treated unfairly.

The assassination of Abdirashid Ali Shermarke ended civilian rule in Somalia. Government leaders tried to pick a new president, but they couldn't agree. Early in the morning of October 21, 1969, the army took over the country, and its commander, General Muhammad Siad Barre, became president. He chaired a Supreme Revolutionary Council (SRC), composed of about two dozen military officers, that ruled the country.

A Socialist State

The aim of the new government was to drastically change Somalian society. Democracy was abolished, and the country's freely elected National Assembly was dissolved.

Neighbors at War

At the beginning of this century, the region between the Juba River in what is now Somalia and the Tana River in Kenya was called Trans-Juba. Even though Somalis were the most numerous people in the region, British colonial authorities claimed Trans-Juba was part of Kenya. The issue was finally resolved by dividing Trans-Juba in half with a boundary that is today the border between Kenya and Somalia.

The division left large numbers of Somalis as residents of a part of Kenya called the Northern Frontier District (NFD). The district is a semidesert, with vast barren plains. It is a harsh, desolate land that tests the survival of the people who live there. Virtually the only vegetation is scattered bush.

Somalis in the NFD felt much closer ties with the Somalis living across the new border than with Kenya. The British reinforced the feelings of the NFD Somalis that they were different from the rest of Kenya's peoples. British authorities would not allow Somalis to travel into the rest of Kenya, and Somalis were taxed much more than other African groups in the colony.

In 1961, during talks in London leading to Kenyan independence, Somalis from the NFD demanded that it be separated from Kenya before the colony became independent. A commission appointed by the British documented that the vast majority of people living in the NFD supported separation from Kenya and unification with the newly independent Somalia. However, the British government did not encourage separation. After Kenya gained its independence in 1963, its government strongly opposed giving up any of its land to Somalia.

By 1963, Somalian guerrilla bands were operating in the NFD. The rebels, armed with various weapons from Communist allies, waged hit-and-run attacks against Kenyan forces. Somalis frequently planted land mines along the desert trails that were used by the Kenyans.

The Kenyan government claimed the rebels had been armed and trained by Somalia with the help of the USSR. The government of Somalia denied the charges but openly supported the guerrillas.

Kenyan army troops and police battled with the guerrillas for four years. The rebellion failed, and in 1967, Somalia's newly elected government smoothed relations with Kenya by accepting the NFD border, thus ending fears that the two countries would continue to clash.

Border problems between Somalia and Ethiopia, however, did lead to serious fighting between these two countries in 1964. The conflict had its roots in borders that had been established between the two countries by the British before Somalia became an independent nation.

Somalia did not recognize borders that gave Ethiopia regions, such as the Ogaden and the Haud, where Somalis were the majority. About half a year after Somalian independence, armed Somalian nomads were clashing with Ethiopian troops in the Haud. For the most part, the clashes stemmed from disputes over issues such as tax collecting. Gradually, however, nationalistic sentiments heated up on both sides of the Somalia-Ethiopia border.

Government radio in both countries blared propaganda against each other. The clashes continued and eventually grew in scope. Violence broke out between Somalian and Ethiopian troops. In February 1964, fighting spread all along the border between the two countries, with Ethiopian aircraft raiding targets far within Somalia.

The conflict threatened stability throughout all of northeastern Africa. The Organization for African Unity and the Democratic Republic of the Sudan arranged a cease-fire between Somalia and Ethiopia, which agreed to end radio propaganda. A joint commission was established to investigate border incidents, and a demilitarized zone was set up six to nine miles deep on each side of the border.

As it did with Kenya, the Somalian government that had been elected in 1964 succeeded in improving relations with Ethiopia. The border remained relatively calm until the Marxist government came to power in Ethiopia during 1974, giving rise to further conflicts and tensions.

Important individual rights, such as freedom of speech, were restricted. Many people who criticized the government were arrested, and some were executed. Siad Barre also arrested political leaders from the old government and outlawed political parties. Private business was limited, although not eliminated. The name of the country was changed from the Somali Republic to the Somali Democratic Republic, which was declared a "socialist state." It was modeled after Communist countries such as the former Soviet Union and China, but there were differences. One of the most important differences was that the Siad Barre government did not discourage religion, although only Islam was recognized by the state.

While Siad Barre may not have discouraged religion, he did try to modify its political influence in Somalia and in doing so suppressed opposition from religious leaders. In 1975, for example, after he had given women equal inheritance rights with men, twenty-three members of the clergy opposed the new law, which went counter to the

Abdirashid Ali Shermarke (left) listens as U.S. president John F. Kennedy welcomes him to Washington, D.C., in 1962. Seven years later, after Shermarke had become the president of Somalia, he was assassinated by a rebel clan member.

Islamic belief that women are not to be treated equally with men. Siad Barre had them arrested, and ten of them were publicly executed. In addition to extending this right to women, Siad Barre gave them political positions in his government and in general increased their participation in society.

By 1976, the SRC was dissolved and replaced by the Somali Revolutionary Socialist Party (SRSP), under the control of Siad Barre. Three years later, the party allowed elections for a People's Assembly, similar to a parliament. However, there was only one political party, the SRSP, and power remained in the hands of a small SRSP committee—five military officers headed by Siad Barre.

The Soviets and the Somalis

While the Somalis had some ties to the Soviet Union before the revolution, the Soviets actually had little influence in Somalia during that period. West Germany and the United States had been providing funds for the Somalian police. Moreover, Somalia had favored the West for some time. Shortly after gaining its independence, Somalia turned to the United States when it wanted to build an army of 20,000. Because the United States was supplying arms to Ethiopia, Somalia's ancient enemy, it offered only 5,000 men. The Soviets offered more support, and the Somalis took it.

After the revolution, the relations between Somalia and the USSR changed even more. Under the Siad Barre government, the Soviet Union became Somalia's most important ally. The Soviets supplied most of the weapons for Somalia's armed forces and trained their officers. By 1976, the Soviet Union had a thousand military advisers in Somalia.

The Soviets also improved and operated a naval base on Somalia's Indian Ocean coast. The base belonged to Somalia, but in reality it was a Soviet installation. Scores

At Odds Over Ivory

Somalia and Kenya have been at odds with each other over more than just land. During the 1970s and 1980s, the number of African elephants in Kenya dropped from 167,000 to 16,000. Most of the elephants were killed for their valuable ivory tusks by poachers, many of whom were armed with automatic rifles. Kenyan officials blamed the Somalis for most of the poaching, a tactic they suspected was being used to create unrest in their country. Somalian poachers also turned to banditry, sometimes wounding or killing tourists, Kenya's chief source of money from abroad. In August of 1989, Somalian bandits in northeastern Kenya killed famed conservationist George Adamson, the husband of the late Joy Adamson, heroine of the book and film *Born Free*. Banditry by Somalis has continued in Kenya.

Officials stand with seven tons of ivory tusks that were confiscated from the largest illegal ivory-poaching operation in African history.

of Soviet naval vessels visited Somalia, and many were stationed offshore.

Somalia is in a very strategic position. Its ports provide Soviet warships access to the Persian Gulf's oil-tanker lanes. And, on the tip of the Horn of Africa, Somalia points directly toward the strife-torn Middle East.

The United States worried about the Soviet presence in Somalia. Somalia walked a tightrope; it continued to take Soviet help, but it did not take orders from Moscow. Then, in 1974, something happened in Ethiopia that caused a split between Somalia and the Soviets.

Friends Again: Somalia and the United States

On September 12, 1974, the emperor of Ethiopia, Haile Selassie, was dethroned by a military coup (overthrow of the government). The new rulers, like the Siad Barre government, looked to the Soviet Union for help.

The United States had been an ally of Ethiopia, but it did not support the new government. The Soviets did and in 1977 agreed to provide Ethiopia with aid.

It was a strange situation for the Soviets. Both Somalia and Ethiopia were Soviet allies, but the two countries were at odds over the Ogaden, the large eastern region of Ethiopia peopled mostly by Somalis. In 1977, Somalia

During conflicts with Ethiopia in 1977, many thousands of refugees poured into Somalia from the Ogaden region. Here, refugee children gather together in a crude Somalian camp.

invaded the disputed region, laying claim to it. The new Ethiopian government reacted strongly and attacked the Somalian rebels. The Soviets—as well as Cuba—provided aid to Ethiopia, which regained control of the area. In retaliation for their support to Ethiopia, Soviet forces were expelled from Somalia.

Huge numbers of Somalian refugees from the Ogaden fled the fighting and poured into Somalia. Others sought refuge in Somalia because the Ogaden was gripped by a fierce drought. Somalia could not handle the millions of refugees. Having expelled the Soviets, Somalia could no longer count on them for help, so it turned to the United States. The United States jumped at the opportunity and supplied Somalia with military and economic aid in return for the use of seaports and airfields. Somalia's path had turned again.

Somalian rebels stand watch at an SNM outpost in Mogadishu. The country's rebel movement, which began in 1981, gained great strength with the collapse of President Siad Barre's government in 1991.

Chaos and Crisis

Siad Barre's government remained in power until January 1991, but its fall had begun almost ten years earlier. Poverty, worsened by drought, had caused widespread dissatisfaction among Somalis. In addition, the clans were enraged because Siad Barre had packed the government with members of his own clan, the Marehan, a small group numbering only 1 percent of the country's population.

In 1981, a rebel movement began in the northern part of Somalia. Most of the rebels belonged to the large Isaaq clan centered there. The rebels named themselves the Somali National Movement (SNM).

Somalia's old enemy, Ethiopia, hoping to destabilize Siad Barre's government, encouraged the SNM. The Ethiopians gave the rebels bases within their borders, in the Ogaden. Somalian government troops and the Ethiopians fought ferociously along the border. The United States airlifted $5.5 million in military equipment to Somalia and sent in military advisers.

During the mid-1980s, the SNM rebellion strengthened. Then Siad Barre brutally cracked down on the rebels. His army leveled entire Isaaq villages and arrested prominent members of the clan. Army artillery pounded the northern capital of Hargeisa, and troops massacred and tortured thousands of unarmed Isaaq civilians.

Meanwhile, violence and unrest spread to other parts of the country. Riots erupted in cities, law and order began to break down, bandits roved the countryside, and clans attacked one another. New rebel movements also began in the southern part of the country.

Since most Somalis barely produce enough food in the best of times, the fighting, which had cut off their food supplies, made things worse. Already suffering from a severe drought, they began to starve.

In May of 1988, the SNM mounted an offensive in the north and captured Hargeisa. Before long, the rebels controlled much of the countryside.

Fall of the Siad Government

By 1989, rebel movements in southern Somalia were gaining ground. One movement was the United Somali Congress (USC), composed mainly of the Hawiye clan. The other was the Somali Patriotic Front (SPF), with a power base in the Ogadeni clan. Ogadenis also were the backbone of the Somalian army, and many began to desert. Smaller rebel movements were formed by still other clans. On September 8, 1989, the U.S. State Department warned that Somalia was in "disintegration."

During months of fierce fighting, rebels, especially the USC, drove for the capital of Mogadishu, entering the city in December 1990. Bloody street fighting followed. Siad Barre's prized troops, the Red Berets, resisted the rebels, but their resistance gradually crumbled.

On New Year's Eve, Siad Barre fled his presidential palace. He eventually headed to southern Somalia and later went to Nigeria. Muhammad Ali Mahdi, head of the

Muhammad Ali Mahdi, the leader of the United Somali Congress, assumed the presidency of Somalia after Siad Barre fled.

Double Duty

In 1991, rebel forces destroyed the former residence of President Siad Barre after they had driven him into exile.

Shortly after Siad Barre fled the presidential palace on December 31, 1990, gunmen besieged the U.S. embassy in Mogadishu. Inside were more than two hundred men, women, and children. Some of them were embassy staff; others were foreign diplomats and Somalian embassy employees. Some had their families with them.

For the gunmen, the embassy was a prize to be looted. They surrounded it and fired machine guns, grenades, and mortar shells. The embassy's small security staff knew it could not hold out long.

The U.S. ambassador contacted Washington, asking that the embassy be evacuated. Because of the fighting, transport aircraft could not land at the city's airport. There was only one solution—helicopters, but the helicopters were on two U.S. ships stationed off Oman, on the other side of the Arabian peninsula, more than a thousand miles away. The ships, and the troops aboard them, were involved in Operation Desert Shield, the first phase of U.S. response to the Iraqi invasion of Kuwait.

On January 2, 1991, the ships U.S.S. *Guam* and U.S.S. *Trenton* headed for Mogadishu, hoping to arrive by January 6. Would they make it in time? Probably not, military commanders reasoned, so on January 3 they placed two Super Stallion helicopters aboard the *Guam* to undertake the five-hundred-mile rescue mission.

U.S. marines operated the helicopters, each of which carried thirty combat marines and nine navy SEALS. Fueled in mid-air, the helicopters whirred into Mogadishu at dawn. As the helicopters landed, looters were trying to climb the embassy walls. The arrival of the American troops sent them running. Marines and SEALS took up defensive positions. The two helicopters were loaded with the first batch of evacuees and returned to their ships.

On January 6, additional helicopters arrived to evacuate the remaining people in the embassy. With them went the last of the marines and SEALS, who returned to their original job, the rescue of Kuwait. They had served double duty.

General Muhammad Farah Aidid heads the Habir Gedir clan, which split off from the USC.

USC, assumed the presidency. A USC plan called for him to govern for two years, after which time elections would be held.

Before the new government was organized, however, a split occurred in the USC. Ali Mahdi belonged to the Abgals subclan of the Hawiye. Another subclan, the Habir Gedir, was led by General Muhammad Farah Aidid. These men were the two most powerful warlords in the USC and in the country. They argued over power, and fighting broke out among their followers.

The two warlords divided Mogadishu in half. Ali Mahdi took over the northern part of the city; his rival took the south. Their gunmen battled continuously, killing many civilians in the cross fire.

Elsewhere in the country, things were not much better. Somalia fell into a state of lawlessness.

The Warlords

After Siad Barre was overthrown, and the country found itself without a government, Somalia was controlled by a number of warlords. Following are brief descriptions of the country's four most powerful warlords.

General Muhammad Farah Aidid, a former army general who trained for the military in Italy, was the strongest warlord. He controlled the central part of the country. Aidid had been a high-ranking official in Somalia's government before he split with Siad Barre, who sent him to jail for a ten-year period in 1965. He was also an ambassador to India.

Muhammad Ali Mahdi controlled part of Mogadishu and a small area around it. However, because he headed the main faction of the USC, he was almost as powerful as Aidid. Before seizing power, he was a wealthy businessman and hotel owner.

Colonel Muhammad Omar Jess, a member of the large Darod clan, ruled the city of Kismayu in southwestern Somalia. He was an ally of Aidid's.

General Muhammad Said Hersi, also known as Morgan, controlled most of southwestern Somalia. A Darod, he is the son-in-law of Siad Barre and was hostile to the rebel clans.

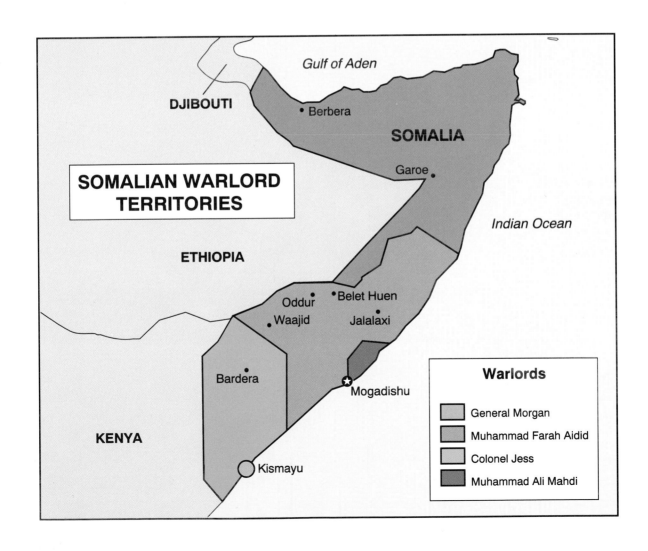

Chapter 3

Problems With Aid

The internal chaos caused by the fall of the Siad Barre government in January 1991, combined with the long-standing drought, which destroyed many farms and herds, caused famine in Somalia. In response to this situation, a relief effort was mounted by various world organizations.

The 1991 Relief Effort

The Red Cross and its Islamic counterpart, the Red Crescent stepped in to help the starving Somalis. They were joined by other agencies, such as Save the Children, CARE, and the United Nations World Food Program. But the gangs waged war on these relief organizations, taking food and medical supplies from their trucks and warehouses at gunpoint. Fighting between gangs often made it impossible to unload supplies from the few ships that docked in Mogadishu, and supplies that did land were frequently stolen at dockside. Some officials estimated that 80 percent of food arriving in Somalia ended up in the hands of the gangs.

As a result, the relief effort fell apart. In December, a Red Cross worker was fatally shot as he tried to hand out

> Heavily armed gangs prevented food and medicine from reaching Somalia's sick and starving.

Opposite:
Outside a hospital in Mogadishu, a Habir Gedir fighter sits atop a pickup truck that is armed with machine guns.

food in Mogadishu. Shortly afterward, sixty tons of food were looted from a Red Cross warehouse, the last of the Red Cross food stockpile.

Help on Hold

The world talked about helping Somalia, but large-scale help was on hold. There were many reasons for the delay. The United States and its allies had just fought a war with Iraq. Moreover, the attention of Western countries was focused on the civil war in the European nation that was once Yugoslavia. As a result, some critics in developing countries charged that the West was not concerned with suffering in a black African land. (Once Operation Restore Hope began, however, other critics claimed that Yugoslavia was being ignored in favor of Somalia.)

The situation grew confused. A few officials in the U.S. State Department wanted to bring the issue of Somalia to the U.N. Security Council, but the Bush administration was against it. At the same time, the United States was critical of the United Nations for not acting. The relief agencies that had tried to help in Somalia had begged the United Nations for assistance. The United Nations, however, had evacuated its people from Mogadishu in January of 1991 and felt that it was too dangerous to send them back.

Boutros-Ghali Steps In

In January 1992, Boutros Boutros-Ghali, Egypt's former deputy prime minister of foreign affairs, became secretary general of the United Nations. He was committed to stopping the fighting and feeding the starving in Somalia. Under his leadership, the United Nations finally began to act. In February, it arranged a truce between the two warring Somalian leaders, Farah Aidid and Ali Mahdi, so relief efforts could be resumed.

Opposite:
A starving woman sits with her children in a small village near Baidoa. Hundreds of thousands of Somalis starved during 1991 and 1992 as international humanitarian efforts were blocked by conflicts among Somalia's rival clans.

The Humanitarian From Egypt

Boutros Boutros-Ghali started a five-year term as U.N. secretary general on January 1, 1992. He was born in Egypt on November 14, 1922, of a well-known and fairly wealthy family. After studying at the University of the Sorbonne in Paris, France, and at Columbia University in New York City, he became a law professor and a journalist. He served as Egypt's minister of state for foreign affairs and deputy prime minister of foreign affairs, and as such was instrumental in smoothing relations between Egypt and Israel.

Boutros-Ghali has always had a keen interest in black African countries. In 1990, his constant efforts and influence encouraged South Africa to release Nelson Mandela from prison. Mandela had been jailed for his activities as a leader against his country's policy of apartheid (racial segregation). As U.N. secretary general, Boutros-Ghali pushed strongly for swift international action in Somalia. Without his efforts, Operation Restore Hope might never have been undertaken.

Boutros Boutros-Ghali

Unfortunately, the truce was shaky. Fighting kept erupting, and looting continued. In April, the U.N. Security Council voted to send fifty unarmed military observers, from Pakistan, to Somalia. Their job was to monitor the truce, but they had no power to do anything about violations.

The Security Council hoped to send five hundred armed Pakistani peacekeepers to protect food that was expected to arrive in Mogadishu, but the United States initially fought the idea for financial reasons. It pays about one third of the United Nations' peacekeeping costs, more than any other country. The administration argued that Congress would not approve another expensive peace-keeping mission in an election year.

Some African diplomats accused the United States of having a double standard. Why, they asked, did the

United States back 14,000 peacekeepers for Yugoslavia, yet oppose 500 for Somalia? Was it racism? Boutros-Ghali implied that it was, accusing the Western nations of being more concerned with Yugoslavia because it was "a rich man's war."

It seemed to many Somalis that the United Nations was paralyzed, or worse, that it did not care about them. They resented the international organization, even though Boutros-Ghali eventually succeeded in getting the United Nations to take action.

The United States Finally Acts

In August of 1992, the United States started taking decisive action. It began to airlift food from Kenya to Somalia for the Red Cross to distribute there. C-130 aircraft, also known as Hercules transports, from the marines and the air force, carried no armed men and bore the Red Cross emblem.

U.S. marine pilots are trained for war, but the men who flew Hercules transports from Mombassa, Kenya, to Mogadishu were not fighting a human enemy. As one

Hundreds of starving Somalis line up at a refugee feeding kitchen in Baidoa. By August of 1992, some aid had begun to reach the needy as a result of initiatives by the United States and other countries.

young lieutenant put it, "It's not our usual job, but we feel pretty good about it. We're helping people stay alive instead of killing them."

Asked about the danger of landing at an airport that was vulnerable to gunmen, the marines said that they were wary but not worried. "It comes with the territory," one sergeant commented. "There's a risk, but we're in and out. You get used to it."

By September, 500 armed Pakistani peacekeepers sent by the United Nations finally reached Mogadishu on U.S. Air Force planes. A four-vessel U.S. Navy task force, with

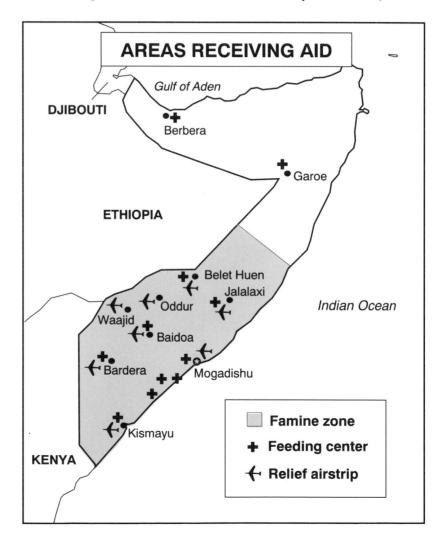

AREAS RECEIVING AID

The Red Cross in Somalia

The 1992 budget for the International Committee of the Red Cross (ICRC) in Somalia was $196 million. Its relief effort was the largest since World War II, involving 106 ICRC delegates and 1,500 Somalian Red Crescent volunteers.

"Dry" rations, such as rice, were given to families to take home. "Wet" rations, including vegetable oil and beans, were cooked at the Red Cross's nine hundred field kitchens and handed out from them.

The kitchens served mainly women, children, and the elderly—those who were most likely to be robbed when carrying home the food. The Red Cross tried to provide two daily meals of 2,400 total calories, including 70 grams of protein, but it was able to achieve only 65 percent of its goal.

The ICRC also provided farmers and herders with seeds and tools. Since December 1991, it has distributed more than 1,260 metric tons of seed, including corn and cowpeas. It has also supplied 18,000 hand tools. ICRC personnel vaccinated more than 2.5 million sheep and goats; 500,000 camels; and 500,000 cattle in 175 villages.

ICRC supplies went to ten hospitals, and its medical teams performed 250 surgeries a week.

2,400 marines, arrived offshore to coordinate the mission. However, once the food arrived, little reached the people. Most was grabbed by the gangs and bandits who were far better armed than the peacekeepers. Meanwhile, the truce between Ali Mahdi and Farah Aidid had long since been broken, and the Somalian people continued to die by the thousands. The situation was no different than before, perhaps even worse.

A young boy, orphaned by the civil war, carries a bowl of rice he received at a feeding center in Mogadishu.

The Celebrity Effort

Many humanitarian efforts have been aided by celebrities whose popularity has enabled them to move those in key positions to focus on important issues. Elizabeth Taylor and Magic Johnson, for example, have used their positions of prominence to help in the fight against AIDS. Two celebrities, the late movie star Audrey Hepburn and former supermodel Iman, brought to the attention of the world the plight of the starving children of Somalia.

Audrey Hepburn, who died in January 1993, had become involved in helping the children of the world before her September 1992 trip to Somalia. In 1988, when she became a special UNICEF (United Nations Children's Fund) ambassador, she went to Ethiopia to aid that country's starving victims. This mission was followed by trips to the Sudan, El Salvador, Guatemala, Honduras, Mexico, Venezuela, Ecuador, Bangladesh, and Vietnam.

Audrey Hepburn knew firsthand what it was like to be hungry and thus could have a greater degree of empathy for the Somalis than many other people. She grew up in Nazi-occupied Holland, where she at one point lived on flour from tulip bulbs. In Somalia, she visited the feeding camps, ministering to the

In September 1992, actress Audrey Hepburn visited Somalian feeding camps and ministered to the starving children.

Somali-born supermodel Iman became actively involved in the effort to help her homeland in 1992 and 1993. Here, she meets with reporters in Washington, D.C., to announce her involvement in planning a National Peace Conference in Somalia.

children. Her work with children was more important to her than movie work. "If I have that kind of energy," she commented, "I must give it to the children."

In October 1992, Iman went to Somalia. Iman Abudulmajid, now a U.S. citizen and wife of rock star David Bowie, was born in Somalia but left there in 1972 for political reasons. Twenty years later, upon returning to her homeland, she found what she described as "skeletal men and women literally wearing sacks," and houses "riddled with bullets."

Before her return, Iman had arranged with the BBC (British Broadcasting Corporation) to make a television documentary of her visit. She felt that a documentary would serve to awaken the world. "People get numbed," she said, "when they see picture after picture, year in and year out, of people starving. I wanted to show that they are not a nation of beggars—that culture, religion, and hope are still there."

During her visit, Iman spent ten days with the BBC camera crew, traveling through the embattled areas of Somalia, risking her life in the hope of spurring the world to action and bringing some measure of comfort to the suffering people of Somalia. "Helping Somalia is going to be a lifetime thing for me," she said.

Chapter 4

Operation Restore Hope Begins

On November 11, 1992, a convoy of thirty-four trucks from Mogadishu rolled across the dusty land toward the city of Baidoa, in central Somalia. Each truck carried eleven tons of wheat, donated by the United States to the United Nations to feed Baidoa's starving people. The trucks had been sent by CARE, which was distributing food in southern Somalia.

Suddenly, from out of the bush, armed bandits attacked. Several Somalis who had been hired as guards and drivers for the convoy were hit, and at least four died. Thirty-three of the trucks turned and fled back over the dusty track toward Mogadishu. Only one truck made it to Baidoa. Meanwhile, the people of Baidoa were dying at a rate of three hundred a day.

The ambush of the CARE convoy was typical of the situation in Somalia. Some food was finally arriving at Mogadishu, but it was still not getting to the starving people. Experts predicted that unless it did, two million Somalis would die within a few weeks.

Increasingly, the media focused on the suffering in Somalia. News coverage put pressure on world leaders. Finally, they faced the fact that the relief effort was doomed without military protection.

In 1992, international forces undertook a mission to help some of the world's neediest people.

Opposite:
American troops received a warm reception from the Somalis when Operation Restore Hope began. Here, a Somalian child walks through the street with a soldier.

Military Protection at Last

The U.S. presidential election was over. The Bush administration was thus free to act on Somalia without worrying about the political campaign. On November 26, George Bush urged that a multinational force—one composed of troops from several nations—be sent to Somalia to guard the relief effort under U.N. sponsorship. He pledged up to 30,000 troops for the mission. The United Nations agreed, and the Security Council empowered the troops to use force if necessary. As it turned out, the Bush administration and Boutros-Ghali differed on how force should be used. The United States felt it should be only a defensive measure. Boutros-Ghali wanted the troops to pacify the country.

On December 3, 1992, the U.N. Security Council voted unanimously to send an American-led military force to Somalia.

More than twenty other countries pledged troops, including France, Belgium, Canada, Saudi Arabia, Italy, Nigeria, the United Arab Emirates, Zimbabwe, Egypt, Botswana, and Australia. Bush welcomed the participation of Islamic and African countries, who made it less likely for Africans to view the mission as an attempt to restore Western colonialism in Somalia.

The U.S. military did not view the warlords and their young thugs as a major threat to its troops. Secretary of Defense Dick Cheney supported this view, saying that he expected little resistance from the untrained and disorganized gangs. Other experts disagreed, including some American diplomats in Africa. They feared that the warlords might take hostages, and their thugs would become terrorists. Writing in the newspaper *USA Today*, Harry Schwartz, a former member of *The New York Times* editorial board, warned that "the American blood toll in Somalia could exceed that of the Gulf War." Critics of the plan cited the Somalis' reputation as tough fighters. One scientist who was born in East Africa of British parents and who has lived closely with native peoples there, warned a reporter: "The Somalis are natural bush fighters. [If] American troops go in, Vietnam could look like a picnic."

The Marines Land

The beginning of the 1992 holiday season was touched with sadness for soldiers at Camp Drum in New York State and marines at Camp Pendleton in California. While other Americans prepared for a festive time with their friends and loved ones, the troops were packing up for Somalia. Aboard the ships of a U.S. Navy amphibious task force off Somalia, four thousand marines were set to go ashore. The crews of heavily armed Cobra attack helicopters had been briefed and ready to provide air support.

Just after midnight on December 9 (Somalian time), the first U.S. troops—20 marine commandos and navy

On December 9, 1992, U.S. marines landed on a beach near the Mogadishu airport to secure the area for the delivery of humanitarian aid.

SEALS— hit the beach next to the Mogadishu airport. Their job was to scout the beach and secure it. Quickly, they took their positions and set up rocket launchers and heavy machine guns. Operation Restore Hope had officially begun.

The advance party of marine commandos and navy SEALS was met by an army of journalists, who had been encouraged by military commanders to cover the landing in order to promote the cause of military spending. Their coverage of the event, however, was criticized by military authorities, who complained that the journalists had endangered the landing party.

A group of 1,800 marines followed the advance party. Going ashore on landing craft and helicopters, they quickly secured the harbor and airport. Then they moved into the city and set up headquarters in the abandoned U.S. embassy. In the days that followed, more marine and army troops landed. Eventually, about 25,000 American troops were stationed in Somalia. Other countries contributed more than expected—7,000 in all.

Desk Marine and Field Marine

General Robert B. Johnston (left)

U.S. marines sometimes place themselves in two categories, desk marines and field marines. A desk marine is an administrator, good at coordination and planning, while a field marine goes out in the mud and puts those plans into action. Operation Restore Hope fell under the overall command of fifty-seven-year-old desk marine General Joseph Hoar. He had succeeded four-star army general H. Norman Schwarzkopf as chief of American military operations from the Middle East to Africa. The field marine was Lieutenant General Robert B. Johnston, who commanded American troops operating in Somalia.

Hoar, who was born in Boston, Massachusetts, joined the U.S. Marine Corps after graduating from college. During the Vietnam conflict, he served as an adviser to the South Vietnamese marines, where he gained a reputation for being an excellent coordinator. This was an important ability during Operation Restore Hope, since Hoar's job involved coordinating the activities of various armed services. It also enabled Hoar to keep track of another tense situation that was going on in Iraq at the same time that Operation Restore Hope was under way.

Johnston, fifty-five, was born in Scotland and came to the United States in 1955, when he was eighteen. Like Hoar, he became a marine after college and served in Vietnam. During Operation Desert Storm, Johnston was chief of staff to General Schwarzkopf. There was speculation among some high-ranking military officers that Johnston might eventually be named commandant of the U.S. Marine Corps.

General Joseph Hoar

Display of Force

Most Somalis welcomed the troops as saviors, cheering them as they went through the streets. The gangs, as was to be expected, were resentful of their presence. The plan of marine commanders was to discourage opposition from the gangs with an overwhelming display of force. Marines on the ground were heavily armed and manifested iron discipline. Overhead, helicopter gunships cruised and hovered, rotors churning the air. The troops made it clear that any attack on them would be met with a thunderous response.

Once the operation was in place, the way in which the United Nations and the United States viewed the role of the troops became an issue. Boutros-Ghali wanted the troops to disarm all gunmen and put down violence of any sort. The United States, on the other hand, said that the troops were not a police force and should fire only if they or relief supplies were menaced. What actually happened was something in between.

At first, U.S. commanders informed the gunmen in Mogadishu that they could continue to carry their light automatic weapons, but they ordered everyone who was carrying heavy weapons off the streets. The weapons quickly disappeared, and Mogadishu grew quiet as the fighting subsided.

Before long, however, violence erupted again, and marine patrols came under fire. It appeared as if the gangs were gathering heavy weapons to use against the troops. The marines and other troops reacted powerfully. When two gangmen fired at Cobra helicopters, the troops blasted their vehicles to scrap, killing several of them. Trucks that ran checkpoints were riddled by fire. When marines came under sniper fire from a compound held by General Farah Aidid's forces, tanks and attack helicopters reduced it to rubble.

Meanwhile, the U.S. special envoy to Somalia, Robert Oakley, worked on a truce between General Aidid and

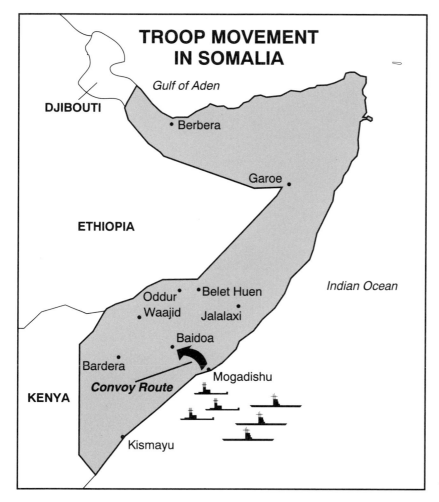

TROOP MOVEMENT IN SOMALIA

Gulf of Aden

DJIBOUTI

• Berbera

Garoe •

ETHIOPIA

Indian Ocean

Oddur •
• Belet Huen

• Waajid
Jalalaxi •

Baidoa
•

Bardera •

Convoy Route

KENYA

Mogadishu

• Kismayu

During Operation Restore Hope, food brought into Somalia by U.S. ships was loaded onto vehicles in Mogadishu. From there, convoys made their way to key cities, the first of which was Baidoa.

Ali Mahdi. The truce was signed on December 11, but periodic fighting continued between them, and against the multinational troops. Other clans, moreover, were not bound by the truce and persisted in making trouble.

As on-again, off-again violence flared, the multinational troops began to act before being attacked. Marines raided sites where gangs had stored heavy weapons, hauling off antiaircraft guns, cannons, and rocket launchers. Nine hundred marines surrounded the Mogadishu market, where guns were being sold like groceries. They made a sweep and loaded several trucks with weapons taken from arms dealers. By February, it appeared that the troops had

Help From the Sea

Operation Restore Hope, plus the operations in Iraq and Bangladesh, proved the value of a new navy-marine corps military strategy to humanitarian efforts. Described as fast-forward deployment from the sea, the strategy is designed for quick response to "small wars" and other crises in any part of the world. Specially trained marine units that are equipped for action are stationed on navy vessels that can be sent forward toward possible trouble spots. As soon as a crisis erupts, the units can move in by air and landing craft to put out the fire before it spreads. If the situation cannot be contained, the marines' mission is to "influence the action" until more military power is brought to bear. As in Operation Restore Hope, the people in these marine and navy units are specialists who work with other branches of the armed services.

made their point. The number of violent incidents and robberies decreased, but they did not end. Every so often, firefights occurred between the troops and the forces of the warlords.

A Strategy for Hope

The first stage of Operation Restore Hope was to establish a safe base for relief supplies in Mogadishu and to get those supplies to the people there. Next, military units were to fan out and protect relief centers in other key cities. After that, heavily guarded relief convoys would be dispatched to them from Mogadishu. Each city would serve as a base from which convoys could then move into the countryside.

The Red Cross, however, preferred to use Somalian guards as a gesture to the Somalis. The presence of the troops still helped, however, by discouraging attacks on Red Cross convoys.

Baidoa was the first target city outside Mogadishu. It had the only other airport in the country for large transport planes. The city was a scene of horror. Gunmen, many of whom had fled there from Mogadishu, killed and robbed at will, but their rule of terror did not last long. U.S. troops helicoptered to an abandoned Soviet air base ninety miles from Baidoa and secured it. From there, more than seventy military vehicles, carrying U.S. marines and Foreign Legionnaires, entered the city. The vehicles were mounted with an array of antitank missile launchers, machine guns, and mortars. Faced with this awesome show of military power, the gunmen disappeared.

The next city on the list was Kismayu, on the coast of southern Somalia. More than two hundred marines moved in by sea, while a hundred Belgian paratroopers dropped on the city's airport. When an outbreak of clan warfare threatened the town, marine Cobra helicopters and Belgian paratroopers pounded warlord forces. Within a few weeks, distribution points had been established in eight key cities. The last to be secured was Belet Huen, guarded by two hundred soldiers of the 87th Infantry Regiment from Fort Campbell, Kentucky, and by forty Canadians.

A Somalian CARE worker hauls a bag of beans to a warehouse in Mogadishu under the armed protection of a U.S. marine.

Bags of food are unloaded from a cargo ship in the port of Mogadishu. By the end of 1992, a network for the delivery of aid was successfully established, and more than 146,000 tons of food had already been sent to Somalia from the rest of the world.

Signs of Hope

While the forces were establishing security, it became apparent that Operation Restore Hope was working. On December 14, 1992, the first relief ship to anchor in Somalia for two months arrived and was unloaded under marine guard. More ships followed. Supplies began to reach distribution points on a regular basis. Every three days, for example, 300 tons of food arrived at Baidoa. By the end of the year 146,000 tons of food had been sent into Somalia from the outside. Ships carried 112,000 tons. Several aircraft provided by the United States, one by Belgium, one by Canada, and another by the Lutheran World Federation carried 19,000 tons. Trucks, entering from Kenya, brought 15,000 tons.

By January of 1993 deaths were decreasing—the death rate in Bardera, another important city, had dropped by 75 percent. In a few areas, repair and rebuilding began, as Somalis started returning to outlying villages.

Meanwhile, Boutros-Ghali had gathered the warlords of fourteen Somali factions in the Ethiopian capital of Addis Ababa. He pressed them to sign a cease-fire and disarm. The warlords indicated they would honor the truce and also agreed to hold a full-fledged peace conference within a short time. But, like everything else in Somalia, the future was uncertain.

To Stay or Not to Stay?

Among the issues that Boutros-Ghali and the United States did not see eye to eye on was the question of how long American troops should remain in Somalia. Boutros-Ghali wanted the Americans to stay until they had restored law and order to the country and had trained a Somalian police force. Once this mission was accomplished, he envisioned lightly armed U.N. peacekeepers moving in to observe and monitor the peace.

Boutros-Ghali's thinking was motivated by the fear that if the gangs were not disarmed, Somalia would again be ravaged by fighting after the Americans had left. Many observers felt likewise and thought that U.S. troops would have to remain for months or possibly longer to prevent a return to chaos.

Rivals Muhammad Farah Aidid (left) and Muhammad Ali Mahdi embrace at a rally that brought the two warlords together to discuss peace. During March and April of 1993, diplomatic efforts continued in an attempt to keep peace between Somalia's longtime warring factions.

The United States wanted to get in, secure the relief effort, and then bring most of its troops home as soon as possible. By mid-January 1993, the American commander, Lieutenant General Robert B. Johnston, said that most of Somalia, except the Mogadishu area, could be turned over to the United Nations a piece at a time. He added that American forces could begin to withdraw gradually.

The United Nations, however, had not even begun to plan the creation of a peacekeeping force, and U.S. officials criticized it for not having done so. The United Nations, charged Representative John P. Murtha of Pennsylvania, was "dragging its feet."

Pressure by the United States for withdrawal increased in February. In Mogadishu, still a trouble spot, small groups of Somalian youths began to harass marines, and confrontations ensued. One thirteen-year-old Somali was killed by marines. Somalian commanders felt that the marines had done their job and could wear out their welcome. It was time to leave, they said.

In early February 1993, U.S. secretary of state Warren Christopher announced that he and U.N. secretary Boutros Boutros-Ghali had agreed on a plan to replace U.S. troops with a U.N. peacekeeping force. This plan, however, did not contain any firm dates for the completion of the transition. Christopher merely said that American troops would be replaced by the U.N. forces "sometime in the relatively near future."

By March, however, it seemed that the plan for troop replacement was beginning its initial stages. Little by little, American troops began to pull out of Somalia, turning over their command to troops from other nations, such as Belgium and Morocco. By mid-March, the number of troops from other nations surpassed the number of American troops in Somalia for the first time since the beginning of Operation Restore Hope. Encourged by the transition, Boutros-Ghali—in something of an "about-face"—predicted that command would be completely turned over to U.N. forces as early as May.

Peacekeepers on a Budget

When first asked about replacing U.S. troops with U.N. peacekeeping forces, Secretary General Boutros Boutros-Ghali was anxious and hesitant. Though many Americans perceived his stance as uncooperative, Boutros-Ghali was worried about the increasing international role the United Nations was being asked to play. The main reason for his concern was the United Nations' relative lack of resources.

In 1993, the United Nations was heavily involved in major efforts in Yugoslavia, Somalia, Cambodia, and El Salvador—as well as in many other countries on a smaller scale. But, according to some analysts, the United Nations was being asked to do much more than it was really capable of financially. "The great powers are loading U.N. peacekeepers well beyond their capabilities," said Barry Blechman, one of the authors of a study on U.N. peacekeeping.

In 1992, U.N. peacekeeping costs rose to almost $2 billion, up from $300 million only five years earlier. To conserve its funds, U.N. headquarters in New York City closed each day at 5 P.M., despite its need to monitor more than a dozen major operations around the globe. In addition, the United Nations could not supply its troops with equipment for the field. Instead, each country was responsible for equipping its own U.N. soldiers, which meant that troops from rich nations were given new uniforms and traveled in armored personnel carriers, while those from poor countries were armed with little more than their rifles and their courage.

Chapter 5

Looking at the Future

Operation Restore Hope was just the beginning of a long process to try to make Somalia a functioning country once again. It would be a major test for the United Nations. The operation also raised hopes that countries around the world could cooperate to help other nations in need.

A New Role for the Military

Operation Restore Hope was the largest humanitarian effort ever undertaken. It was especially meaningful because it involved so many countries working together to use their military forces, not to fight a territorial battle, but to save human lives. This goal pointed to a new role for the military—especially for the American forces, who had led the effort—in the post-Cold War world of the future.

Two smaller humanitarian operations carried out by U.S. forces after the end of the war in the Persian Gulf had set the stage for Operation Restore Hope. One occurred in northern Iraq right after the Gulf War, where hundreds of thousands of Kurd refugees had fled after a rebellion was crushed by Iraqi dictator Saddam Hussein.

Efforts in Somalia paved the way for more military missions of goodwill around the world.

Opposite:
A soldier reaches out from his tank to the hungry children of Mogadishu. Leaders from around the world must decide how best to use their combined military strength for humanitarian purposes in the years to come.

In April 1991, American forces, along with British and French troops, set up refugee camps in northern Iraq. They provided food, clothing, and shelter for 700,000 Kurds and established a security zone to shield Kurdish refugees from Iraqi forces.

A month after the United States had come to the aid of the Kurds, a cyclone swept through the Asian country of Bangladesh. Thousands of people were left homeless, food was scarce, drinkable water supplies were low, communications were downed, and transportation was destroyed. Local authorities could not cope with the disaster by themselves. In response to their plight, the United States sent in a navy task force carrying marines who were on their way home from Operation Desert Storm. The marines led a relief effort that provided water purification, transportation, communications, and medical care to help Bangladesh get back on its feet.

Operation Restore Hope ensured that the starving Somalian people received the food that they so desperately needed, saving perhaps millions of lives. At the same time, however, the undertaking cost lives. Each loss was tragic, but, fortunately, the total number of casualties was relatively small.

The deaths of the Americans and the Somalis that were incurred as a result of Operation Restore Hope served to underscore the new role of the military. In addition, the deaths raised the important question of exactly how far the military should go in its efforts to carry out a humanitarian mission.

Help From Where?

Many Somalis wanted the United States to play a strong role in rebuilding their country's economy and restoring democracy. The United States indicated a willingness to be involved, but it did not want to give the appearance of running Somalia, nor did it want all the responsibility for

Opposite:
American command of Operation Restore Hope was handed over from President Bush to President Clinton in January 1993. The future of U.S. involvement in Somalia, and the future of the American military in the post-Cold War era, will be greatly determined by the Clinton administration.

the job. U.S. government officials therefore called for the United Nations to guide Somalia toward stability and economic reform.

This proposal met with opposition from the Somalis, many of whom distrusted the United Nations. They believed that the U.N. response to Somalia's disaster was weak and confused. Moreover, General Farah Aidid suspected that the United Nations favored his rival, Ali Mahdi and worried that Ali Mahdi might gain U.N. support for his presidency, declared after Siad Barre had fled Somalia.

The United Nations appeared interested in restoring Somalia's government, and it promised to send a large contingent of peacekeeping troops to Somalia after the Operation Restore Hope troops had left the country. The United Nations, however, seemed to be stalling over differences with the United States about the role of the troops. While the debate continued, the fate of Somalia hung in the balance.

A Difficult Road for the Future

Most observers agree that Somalia has a difficult road to travel and will not be able to make it on its own. Because of the severity of its problems, the country will probably continue to require relief supplies and technical assistance for a long time to come. Many Somalis require long-term medical treatment; cities and villages must be rebuilt; and livestock that was lost to drought, famine, and war must be replenished. Basically, the entire Somalian society needs to be patched together.

The beginnings of a new start for Somalia occurred with developments in late March 1993. At the end of a thirteen-day peace conference sponsored by the United Nations in Addis Ababa, Ethiopia, fourteen Somalian warlords agreed to stop fighting and create a transitional government. The signing of a formal agreement followed

A Stronger United Nations for the Future

U.N. peacekeepers are not peacemakers. They are armed, but lightly and only for their own protection. They cannot use force to stop factions, such as the Somalian clans, from fighting. Peacekeepers in Yugoslavia, for instance, have not been able to stop the bloodshed there. They serve mainly as observers and mediators.

In recent years, the United Nations has expanded its peacekeeping role. There are a total of 60,000 peacekeepers stretched thin across thirteen countries of the world. They are dispatched by the U.N. Security Council, unless a member country casts a veto.

Peacekeeping has become expensive. It costs $3 billion a year, about a third of which is paid by the United States. Some members of Congress want to reduce the U.S. share for the future.

Some observers think the rules of peacekeeping are changing and add that the United Nations has not recognized this fact. In the past, the United Nations has run peacekeeping operations on a shoestring budget, using only a handful of people with little or no military experience. Communications were often poor, and intelligence about conditions on the ground was incomplete. But, by March 1993, major plans were under way to vastly improve the operations and international effectiveness of the U.N. peacekeeping efforts.

Boutros Boutros-Ghali, who had strong support, urged more muscle for U.N. peacekeepers. He envisioned a standing force that would be maintained by member countries. Units, which would be on forty-eight-hour call, would have the authority to enforce peace militarily. The U.N. headquarters in New York City would create a twenty-four-hour-a-day "war room" that would be in constant touch with forces around the world and would act as a central "nerve center" for all operations.

The complexity of U.N. involvement in operations for places such as Yugoslavia and Somalia made it clear that U.N. peacekeeping improvements needed to be made. In this way, Somalia actually helped the United Nations to become stronger, rather than the other way around.

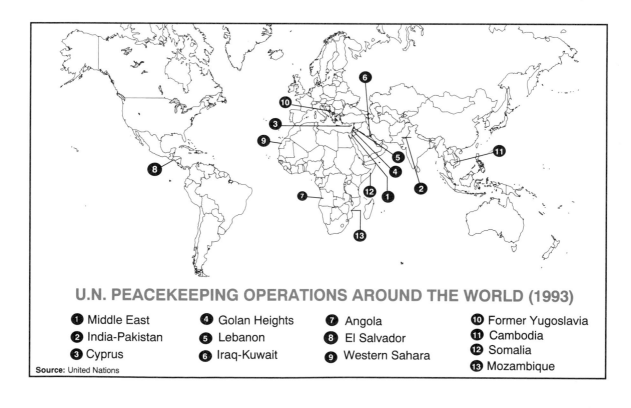

U.N. PEACEKEEPING OPERATIONS AROUND THE WORLD (1993)

1. Middle East
2. India-Pakistan
3. Cyprus
4. Golan Heights
5. Lebanon
6. Iraq-Kuwait
7. Angola
8. El Salvador
9. Western Sahara
10. Former Yugoslavia
11. Cambodia
12. Somalia
13. Mozambique

Source: United Nations

a resolution by the U.N. Security Council to send a force of 30,000 multinational peacekeeping troops to replace the U.S.-led forces in Somalia.

The warlords agreed to disarm within a period of ninety days, and, according to the agreement, violators would be punished with sanctions to be enforced by multinational peacekeepers.

The interim government would be run by a Transitional National Council, which would be made up of seventy-four members, three from each of Somalia's eighteen regions, one from each warlord's faction, with five extra representatives from Mogadishu.

The Transitional National Council was empowered to appoint top government officials and a committee to draw up rules under which the interim government would operate. Also, the council was to create an independent court system, as well as regional and local governing bodies that would be under the supervision of the council.

The future of Somalia's transition government was still uncertain, but almost everyone felt that the agreement was an important and positive step toward long-lasting peace and a new prosperity. Its success would depend on the cooperation and commitment of Somalia's people. If a stable government could be created, Somalia would have a chance, and Operation Restore Hope would be remembered as the start of a new life for the Somalis.

Chronology

1898 In a conflict dubbed the Fashoda Incident, Great Britain and France clash over a trading route running across Africa from Senegal to Somaliland.

Early 1900s Great Britain establishes itself in northern Somalia (British Somaliland), and Italy gains control in southern Somalia (Italian Somaliland).

1948 Britain gives the Ogaden, an area claimed by Somalia and largely populated by Somalis, to Ethiopia, paving the way for future hostilities.

July 1, 1960 British Somaliland and Italian Somaliland become the independent Somali Republic.

1963 In an unsuccessful rebellion that lasts until 1967, Somalia tries to claim northeastern Kenya.

1964 A brief border war erupts between Somalia and Ethiopia. The conflict is temporarily resolved until new fighting begins in the 1970s.

July 1967 Abdirashid Ali Shermarke is elected president of Somalia.

October 15, 1969 Shermarke is assassinated by a rival clan member.

October 21, 1969 The army takes over Somalia, with General Muhammad Siad Barre as its new president. Democracy is abolished, the National Assembly is dissolved, the Supreme Revolutionary Council (SRC) is created, and the country is renamed the Somali Democratic Republic.

1976 The SRC is dissolved and replaced by the Somali Revolutionary Socialist Party (SRSP). The Soviet Union becomes Somalia's most important ally.

1977 Somalia invades Ethiopia's Ogaden. The Soviets aid the Ethiopians, causing the Somalis to expel the Soviets. Somalian refugees from the Ogaden pour into Somalia.

1980s Rebel movements take hold in Somalia: The SNM (Somali National Movement), the USC (United Somali Congress), and the SPF (Somali Patriotic Front).

January 1991	The government of Siad Barre falls.
1991	The Somalis begin to starve as a result of both a drought and chaos caused by the fall of the Siad government, which destroyed many farms and livestock. Efforts by world organizations to get food to the Somalis fail.
August 1992	U.S. efforts to aid the starving Somalis fail in the absence of military protection.
December 3, 1992	The U.N. Security Council unanimously votes to send in an American-led military force to guard relief efforts in Somalia.
December 9, 1992	Operation Restore Hope begins when U.S. troops land on a beach near the Mogadishu airport to secure the area for the delivery of aid.
March 1993	The U.N. Security Council passes a resolution to send a multinational peacekeeping force to replace U.S.-led forces.
	At a U.N.-sponsored peace conference held in Addis Ababa, Ethiopia, Somalian warlords agree to stop the fighting and create a transitional government in Somalia.

For Further Reading

Godbeer, Deardre. *Somalia.* New York: Chelsea House, 1988.

Murray, Jocelyn. *Africa.* New York: Facts on File, 1990.

Ross, Stewart. *United Nations.* New York: Franklin Watts, 1990.

Timberlake, Lloyd. *Famine in Africa.* New York: Franklin Watts, 1986.

Walker, Jane. *Famine, Drought, and Plague.* Chicago: Franklin Watts, 1992.

Index

Photo Credits

Cover: Gamma-Liaison; p. 4: © Van Der Stockt/Gamma-Liaison; p. 6: Wide World Photos; p. 7: Wide World Photos; p. 12: UPI/Bettmann; p. 16: UPI/Bettmann; p. 18: UPI/Bettmann; p. 20: UPI/Bettmann; p. 22: Wide World Photos; p. 23: UPI/Bettmann; p. 24: Wide World Photos; p. 26: Wide World Photos; p. 27: © M. Akin/Gamma-Liaison; p. 28: © Scott Daniel Peterson/Gamma-Liaison; p. 30: Wide World Photos; p. 33: Wide World Photos; p. 34: © Jean-Michel Turpin/Gamma-Liaison; p. 35: Wide World Photos; p. 37: Wide World Photos; p. 38: © Walker Simon/Gamma-Liaison; p. 39: Wide World Photos; p. 40: Wide World Photos; p. 42: Wide World Photos; p. 44: © Van Der Stockt/Gamma-Liaison; p. 45: (top and bottom) Wide World Photos; p. 49: Wide World Photos; p. 50: © Peterson/Gamma-Liaison; p. 52: Wide World Photos; p. 54: © Van Der Stockt/Gamma-Liaison; p. 57: Wide World Photos.

Maps by Sandra Burr and Sean Kelsey.
Special thanks to Cindy Dopkin and Elvis Brathwaite.